DECEPTION

Jenny Penn

EROTIC ROMANCE

Siren Publishing, Inc.
www.SirenPublishing.com

A SIREN PUBLISHING BOOK
IMPRINT: Ménage Amour

DECEPTION
Copyright © 2008 by Jenny Penn

ISBN-10: 1-60601-291-6
ISBN-13: 978-1-60601-291-8

First Printing: November 2008

Cover design by Jinger Heaston
All cover art and logo copyright © 2008 by Siren Publishing, Inc.

Printed in the U.S.A.

PUBLISHER
Siren Publishing, Inc.
www.SirenPublishing.com

DEDICATION

To Michele for reading everything that came before it.

DECEPTION

Jenny Penn
Copyright © 2008

Chapter 1

At the sound of the office doorbell buzzing, Tessa rushed from her attic apartment down to the small entry lobby at the front of her third-floor office space. Panting with exertion, she threw open the frosted glass doors.

Oh, baby! Two of them!

Tessa gaped at the hard-bodied hunks standing in front of her. Construction workers, but not the dirty, nasty type with beer guts and greasy hair. These men were the kind that played in commercials, or movies, or as strippers.

They were masterpieces of hard lines and sharp angles, of rugged jaws and angled cheekbones, thick lashes, piercing eyes, kissable lips; tall, tanned and too handsome to be real. They were perfect.

The one to the right had chocolate-colored hair that contrasted sharply with his midnight blue eyes. His features were drawn tight, closed and remote. An old, faded scar interrupted one of his straight eyebrows and it added to the air of somber danger he emanated.

By contrast, his partner was shorter, thicker and lighter in coloration. His slightly shaggy blond hair gave him a rakish look. The wicked grin playing around the edges of mouth matched his smoky gray eyes, bedroom eyes. This one was definitely a charmer.

"I'm Ty—" The dark one began to introduce himself.

"You two are perfect. The agency couldn't have picked better specimens." Tessa waved her hands with excited nervousness, a giddy giggle escaping.

"Specimens?" The blond cocked an eyebrow. "Do you hear that, Ty? We're specimens."

The dark-haired man scowled. Tessa barely noticed, still overcome by their presence. She'd asked for a hot man and she'd certainly gotten just what she ordered. You didn't find men like this at the supermarket, that was for sure.

"Come on in." Tessa latched onto one thick biceps and couldn't help but give it a squeeze as she pulled Ty through the door. "They're waiting upstairs for you."

"What? Who?" Ty let the strange woman pull him into the darkened office.

This was not the reception he had been expecting. Chase and him had come to Miller's Design in search of Tessa Miller, the wicked witch South Bend. Whoever this woman was, she obviously had them confused with somebody else.

It was apparent Chase was not about to correct her misunderstanding. Not that Ty expected him to do anything else. His best friend since childhood and now business partner, Chase was always getting into mischief.

"I don't know who you are, but I'm looking for Miss Miller. I'm—"

"Oh, I'm sorry." She cut him off again and gave him an engaging double-dimpled grin. "I forgot to introduce myself. I'm Tessa Miller. Now come on, they're waiting to see you."

Chase grinned. Ty knew what he was thinking. This was too good to be true. This pint-sized minx was the witch of South Bend? This was the woman who'd single-handedly brought their multimillion-dollar condominium development to a stop?

Ty was having trouble processing that thought as well. The condo complex was going to be a very profitable investment for Banning & Dunn. All the buildings to the left and right of the building that housed Miller's Design were bought and vacant. The plans were printed, permits in hand. Everything was set for demolition to begin.

That is, everything but Miss Tessa Miller. Never had he run across such a cantankerous renter before. She'd begun her campaign as a series of letters. It had escalated from there when Ty, via their lawyer, had tried to bribe her out of the building.

She had refused the money and been exceedingly rude to Dave, who had then started legal action with unusual zeal. That hadn't intimidated Miss Miller; she had hired her own attack attorney.

Then she had stepped up the heat and contacted the historical society. Now she was not only trying to stop Banning & Dunn from demolishing her building, she was also attempting to stop them from tearing down *any* of the buildings. It was a mess, a disaster, a headache Ty didn't need right now.

That was exactly what had brought them to her door tonight. They were here to try a last-ditch attempt at face-to-face negotiations before the situation dragged on any longer and became more expensive than it already was.

"We were so nervous that the agency wouldn't take our request seriously," Tessa babbled on as she began to physically drag Ty past a series of worktables and storage bins.

"I didn't think the lady on the phone thought I was serious," she confided.

"Why wouldn't she?" Chase asked, playing along.

"She used the word 'unusual,' like, eight times." Tessa waved her hand again, nearly smacking Chase in the process. "But in that way that implies…"

"Disbelief?" Chase suggested.

"More like disgust."

Disgust?

Agencies, specimens, the mysterious 'them,' and now disgust. Whatever was going on, it sounded kind of kinky. Chase liked kinky. He was also liking the wicked witch of South Bend, as he had named her several weeks ago.

Of course, that was before meeting her. She'd earned the name from the sharp, belligerent letters she had written. They had formed an image in Chase's mind of a short hag of a woman, one with a pinched-up face, cold eyes and a large pole permanently protruding directly from her ass.

He had been right about the short part. She barely reached his shoulders, but she wasn't a dainty, waif-like creature either. Soft and gently rounded, she exuded an alluring sweetness that tempted him to take a bite and see if she tasted as good as she looked.

He wondered what her reaction to that would be. The puckered nipples pointing through her blouse said she would gladly return the favor, but there was something about the wild mass of honey curls framing her heart shaped-face with those big, laughing hazel eyes that made her look innocent.

Chase's cock stirred, reminding him that they hadn't done innocent in a while. A long while. Too long, Chase decided as he watched the sway of her generous hips beneath her rumpled skirt as she walked ahead of him through the office, still towing Ty by one muscled arm. He felt his cock harden and pulse with need. Yeah, she had a nice ass, just perfect for holding while he pumped himself fast and furious into her from behind.

From the dent in Ty's Jeans, Chase knew she had the same effect on him. The way Ty was letting the little woman drag him around was telling, too. Of the two of them, Ty was always the controlling, dominant one who made a woman kneel and obey. He had a special room full of toys for just that purpose.

Chase got a thrill out of mastering a woman, but he was willing to follow as well as lead on the occasion. Ty never followed. Chase eyed the small hand that was managing to drag Ty past the workstations. Well, he never had before.

Apparently, he wasn't going to now, either. Chase almost ran into Ty when he dug his heels in. They had reached the door at the back of the office when Ty forced everybody to a standstill.

"Something wrong?" Tessa turned wide eyes and an even wider smile on him.

"Yes, Miss Miller. I'm not sure you—"

"Oh, am I making you uncomfortable?" She let him go. "I'm sorry. I'm being pushy, aren't I? I'm just so excited you showed up, but I assure you there is no need to worry."

"Worry?"

"I promise we'll treat you with the utmost respect. I wouldn't let anybody do anything to you that you are uncomfortable with. To tell the truth, I'm a little nervous myself. I've never done anything like this."

She imparted that last bit in a whisper as she leaned close. Ty got a strong whiff of her lavender-scented hair and for a moment lost his train of thought. Damn, but the woman was confusing him. Not just what she was saying and doing, but his response to her was all wrong.

"We're not going to gangbang you or anything." She patted his arm in reassurance. "You're quite safe."

"Yeah, Ty." Chase snickered. "They're not going to gangbang us, so relax."

Ty shot Chase a hard look, annoyed with him for enjoying this so much. He was annoyed with himself, too, for not being able to get the image of being gangbanged by a group of women led by Tessa Miller out of his mind. The idea made his cock throb with approval.

"We're not expecting anything from you right now. Linda just wanted to check you out before we went over the details of your job," Tessa continued, completely unaware of his distraction.

"Our job?"

"Well, not both of you." Tessa looked between the two men. "That's a little more kinky than I think we're willing to go, but we'll let Linda make the choice."

"Kinky?" Chase grinned. "So, how kinky are you willing to go, sweetheart?"

"Didn't they explain everything to you at the agency?"

"Apparently not."

Chase wondered what this agency was. The idea of a stripper came to mind. Perhaps she was hiring talent for a bachelorette party.

"Well, I'll explain it all, but first let's let Linda get a look at you. She'll know better if you're her husband's type."

Her husband's type?

Chapter 2

Instead of falling down the rabbit hole, Ty walked up a long, narrow flight of stairs and stepped through a dark wooden door into Never-Never Land. Still, he felt his reason and sanity disappear, snatched away by the lovely witch still babbling nonsense.

Tessa bustled around him, latching back onto his arm. The tiny hand had amazing strength as she pulled him into a small dining room and presented him to the two women waiting there.

"Well, what do you think?" Tessa asked Linda and Marcie.

"Damn." Marcie grinned and rose. "How much does he cost?"

"Stop it, Marcie." Tessa laughed, letting go of her hostage. "You're not desperate enough to spend fifteen hundred dollars for a night with a prostitute."

"Prostitute?" Ty's mouth nearly fell open at that bit of information. "Excuse me?"

"Oh, I'm sorry." Tessa blushed. "I meant escort."

"Fifteen hundred, huh?" Marcie eyed the hunk glaring at Tessa. "Depends on what kind of tricks he does."

"Kinky slut," Tessa teased her longtime friend.

"I'm not the one with rings on her bed, sweetheart."

"Yeah, but you are the one who gave them to me for Christmas," Tessa shot back.

"Well, well, well." Marcie circled the blond Adonis who had stepped into the room behind them. "What is this? A buy one-get one free sale?"

"A two-for-one special." Tessa snickered.

"Nice boner." Marcie's hand darted out to cup the brunette's obvious bulge.

"Hey, now!" Ty stumbled backward, displeased with the woman's boldness.

"Keep your hands off the men." Tessa grabbed Marcie by the shoulder and forced her back around the table.

"Wait a minute!" Marcie jerked out of Tessa's hold and turned on the two men, "I'm not done looking."

"I told them they wouldn't be molested on sight." Tessa latched back onto her friend.

"Too bad, I wouldn't mind a free sample."

"Sit!" Tessa pointed to Marcie's chair.

When she was seated, Tessa turned to the third woman in the room. The skinny blonde had kept her head down, but Ty could see her face was bright red. Her obvious embarrassment was to her credit, as far as he was concerned.

"Okay, Linda. Which one do you think Henry will like?"

"I don't know about this, Tessa." Linda peeked from under her lashes, pointedly keeping her eyes away from the men.

"Oh, honey." Tessa moved quickly to put an arm around her friend. "I know this is difficult for you, but you need to know the truth."

"Yeah, Lin." Marcie nodded. "If your old man is out there banging other men, you got a problem."

"Oh, God." Linda buried her face in her hands.

"Marcie!" Tessa glared at her friend. "A little tact?"

"Tact?" Marcie snorted. "I'm not the one that hired the prostitutes."

"They're cheaper than a private eye."

Ty could not believe what he had just heard. Of all the insane, ludicrous things he had ever heard, Tessa Miller took the cake. That was saying something, given some of the moronic ideas Chase had come up with over the years.

Ty barely paid attention as Tessa and her friend, Marcie, continued to console the weeping blonde. He had to figure out a way to set Tessa Miller straight. He wondered what her reaction would be.

Most people would be horribly embarrassed and want to keep the incident quiet. He doubted Tessa would respond the way most people did. He was determined to find out as Marcie led Linda through the kitchen and out the back door that led to the old wrought iron fire escape that functioned as the small apartment's private entrance.

"Listen, Miss Miller, I think there has been a mistake here. We're not prostitutes."

"Speak for yourself," Chase butted in. "I'm more than willing to give Miss Miller a free sample."

"Shut up, Chase!"

"Don't worry." Tessa patted Ty on the arm, drawing his narrowed gaze back to her. "I know. You're an escort. That's all we're paying you to do, escort. Anything else is, well, that's your personal business, though I would consider it a favor if you didn't … do anything with Henry."

"You would?"

"I'd feel awfully bad if I set up Linda's husband to cheat on her. That's just sort of sick, you know?"

"That's what you think is sick?"

Tessa blushed. "Oh, jeez. I just keep putting my foot in my mouth. I didn't mean anything by that."

"Of course not," Chase assured her.

"There's nothing wrong with being gay or anything."

"No there isn't," Ty agreed.

"I'm perfectly fine with it. Not that I've ever, you know, tried it that way."

"Maybe you should," Chase suggested. Now there was an image. Tessa didn't appear to have heard him, but his dick certainly had.

"Even if you were a woman, I wouldn't want you to sleep with Henry. That would hurt Linda and we just want to know if, well …"

"If he's gay," Ty filled in for her.

"Technically, bisexual."

"Bisexual?" Ty blinked as the conversation became weirder. Tessa Miller was insane; cute, but loonier than a cuckoo clock.

"Well, because he's married to a woman, he can't be totally gay." Tessa paused as if considering what she had just said. "I mean, not only gay. Whatever. You know what I mean. Anyway, I'm going to have to pick between you two."

"Pick me."

"What?" Ty's mouth fell open at Chase's offer.

"He's a stick in the mud." Chase jerked his head toward Ty.

"I am not!" Why the hell was he arguing about this?

"No fun at all."

"Really?" Ty turned to confront his aggravating friend. "What about Lisa—"

"Gentlemen!" Tessa clapped her hands together, drawing their attention back to her.

"Sorry, Tessa." Chase stepped closer to the little woman, causing his cock to push painfully against his slacks. He was already mentally betting himself how long it would take him to get her naked.

"You don't mind if I call you Tessa, do you?" Chase used his most seductive drawl.

"That's fine." She patted him on the chest. "But I'm afraid that I'm going with the other gentleman."

"What?" This time it was Chase's jaw that dropped.

"Gee, I'm overwhelmed with gratitude."

"I'm sorry, Chase, was it? Henry likes, well, refined things. And while you are quite attractive, you're a little more bulky—"

"Are you calling me fat?"

"Thick."

"Thick?"

"There is nothing wrong with your body, I'm sure you don't have much body fat."

Tessa eyed his heavily muscled body and felt a shiver pass over her. Definitely not much fat, but the man wasn't paying attention to her look. He was still stuck on indignant.

"Less than six percent."

"Six percent?" Tessa blinked.

"Body fat. Less than six percent body fat."

"You know that?" Ty stared at Chase as if he had grown a second head.

"You don't?"

"No. I don't walk around with my measurements memorized. I'm not a woman."

"What the hell do you mean by that?"

"Gentlemen! I don't have time for a lovers' spat. Can we—"

"A what?"

"He's not my lover." Chase gave Ty a superior look. "I could do better than him."

"In your dreams."

"Please, you can't even afford to keep a man like me."

"I wouldn't want to!"

"Gentlemen!" Tessa clapped her hands, bringing their glares back to her. "Thank you. Now, do you own a suit?"

"Me?" Ty blinked. At her nod, he snorted. "I might have one."

"It's not cheap." Tessa cringed at the word. "Is it?"

Chase bit back his laughter. "Oh, God. This is too weird."

"I have a nice pinstriped one." Ty knew it then. He'd caught the disease. Tessa wasn't just out of her mind. She was contagious.

"You're too thick for pinstripes."

"I am not." It was a damn handmade suit and he looked fabulous in it, turned women's heads. Hell, he turned men's heads too.

"Perhaps, we could just get you a pair of charcoal slacks and a nice sweater that matches your hair. You have beautiful hair."

"Thank you. I think." Ty wasn't sure if being called beautiful was a compliment for a man, since nobody had ever called him that.

"It's very thick and the color is amazing, but it's a little long."

"It is?"

"Maybe some fake glasses will help make you look more scholarly and less, well construction."

Ty took a deep breath. His fascination with Tessa and her strange comments aside, he needed to be an adult and set her straight.

"I think we need to discuss something a little more pertinent than glasses and haircuts."

"Really? What?"

"We're not what you think we are."

"I'm sure most of your jobs are just to escort women or men to functions and be a pleasant date." Tessa spoke quickly, fearing they were trying to back out of the job. "I imagine this would be a little disconcerting for you. Don't worry. It's all aboveboard. Henry is not going to come after you, so don't sweat it."

"Yeah, Ty. It's all aboveboard, so loosen up."

"Chase!"

"Here." Tessa held out a photograph, a wedding picture, to be exact. Ty stared at it in confusion.

"What is that?"

"A picture of Henry."

"What do I want that for?"

"So you know who to hit on."

"I'm not gay!"

"It's all right if you are."

She gave him a condescending pat on the arm that made Ty's teeth grind together. He was hard, painfully so thanks to the nut job in front of him, and she was insisting on setting him up with a man. It was more than he could take. There was one way to prove the point to her.

Without a word, he grabbed Tessa's shoulders and yanked her close until her soft breasts flatted against his chest. He caught a glimpse of her startled expression right before his kissed her.

Chapter 3

Tessa was shocked when Ty's mouth covered hers. Too stunned to respond, she offered no resistance as his tongue slid between her lips. Then it was too late.

He tasted like well-aged bourbon, hot and potent. The flavor drugged her, sucking her beneath an onslaught of desire as his velvety tongue took command of her mouth. The kiss was hot, hard, demandingly male. Tessa was helpless to do anything but respond.

Drunk on the delicious taste of him, she tangled her tongue with his, taunting him with quick, playful thrusts, trying to push his tongue from her mouth till he muttered a curse and savagely fought back.

The kiss exploded beyond mere mouths as Tessa's arms wrapped around his broad shoulders. Her nails dug into his hard muscles as she pressed her body tightly against his. Ty's hands reciprocated the gesture, biting into the soft flesh of her hips and yanking her close so his large erection could grind against her rounded stomach.

Chase blinked, not quite believing what he was seeing as he watched Ty devour Tessa's mouth.

Well, shit. If he's going to get some, I'm going to get some too.

It wasn't like his dick wasn't hard thanks to the pint-sized woman Ty had crushed in his arms. The wicked witch of South Bend was definitely a delectable beauty. One that should be shared between friends.

Ty knew he should stop before things got out of control, but then he felt Tessa being pressed even more firmly against him. He lifted his head, caught the heated look in Chase's eyes and knew there was no stopping now.

Before Tessa could recover from the overwhelming effect of Ty's kiss, her head was being turned and another set of hard lips were pressing into her already swollen ones. Chase's kiss was different, but no less devastating.

Instead of the savage dominance of Ty's, Chase's kiss was flirty. His tongue danced through her mouth as he explored her. She almost felt like giggling as he teased the sensitive recesses of her mouth.

However lighthearted Chase's kiss was, there was nothing playful about the way he was pressing her into Ty. Tessa couldn't stop her body from arching into the feel, trying impossibly to get closer to both men. The two hard, hot male bodies rubbing against her made her breasts swell, the tips becoming painfully sensitive as the fabric of her bra rasped over them.

Ty could feel the hard peaks poking against his chest and was consumed with the desire to see them, touch them, taste them. Too many tiny buttons barred his way. Growling with impatience, he ripped the fabric out of his way, sending buttons flying everywhere.

Leaning back, he looked down at the generous globes straining against her bra. His mouth went dry at the sight of her pink nipples peeking out through the lacy cups. They were puckered, demanding attention and with a groan, he cupped her swollen breasts, teasing and tormenting the harden buds through the sheer fabric.

It wasn't enough. He wanted, needed, to see the pink little buds. He fumbled with the front clasp of her bra, finding his normally adept hands clumsy and shaky. A giggle drew his gaze up and he found Tessa grinning at him. Chase's head was resting on Tessa's shoulder, a wicked gleam in his eye.

"I think he needs help," Chase commented as he began to nibble on Tessa's neck.

"Isn't it bad form for a prostitute not to know how to undo a bra?"

"He's in training."

"That's apparent. He tore my shirt."

"Deduct it from his tip."

Ty was not in the mood to play or be played with. He was on fire, the inferno more intense than it had ever been. His cock pounded like an angry beast against the confines of his jeans. The pressure from the restricting denim made his balls feel like they would explode if his swollen flesh was not soon released.

"You can deduct this too," Ty growled, tearing her bra open.

Tessa's laughter dissolved into a moan as his work-roughened hands cupped her soft flesh. His thumbs rubbed her nipples back and forth, slowly driving her insane. She could not take such gentle teasing and she wound her hands into his hair, pulling his head demandingly down to her breast.

Ty gave in to her silent command and carefully, teasingly lapped at her nipple. The motion tickled and a rough, guttural laugh was torn from her throat as she forced her breast up, pushing her nipple against his lips.

"Please."

Ty's restraint broke. He gave in to his hunger, sucking her hardened tip deep into his mouth. She writhed and moaned against him. She was so sweet, so responsive it drove the need riding him higher, unleashing his bestial nature. As he moved from one breast to the other, he used his fingers, tongue, lips and teeth to torment her sensitive flesh.

Chase groaned as he watched Ty love Tessa's breast. He wanted a taste, wanted to taste her all. With that single intent, he slid his hands down over the generous curves of her hips, snatching the zipper of her skirt and undoing it.

The skirt fell to the floor, leaving only a pair of flimsy, lace panties in his way. Not about to be outdone by Ty's barbarian techniques, Chase tore the underwear from her body. Forcing his hand between Ty and Tessa, he boldly cupped her mound.

Tessa groaned. The small part of her brain trying to warn her that this was wrong was choked by the erotic sensations of having one man licking her tits while another's fingers traced over the edges of her pussy lips. One thick finger divided her folds and slid up the center of her slit, making her arch and moan. Her legs parted to allow his questing fingers further access.

She was as wet as Chase had thought she would be. When he felt her clit beneath his finger, he flicked it, making her cry out, her hips arching into his touch.

Tessa had never felt so good. A delicious coil of tension began wrapping around her pussy, spreading out over her belly, twirling and strengthening with the sparkly pleasure radiating from her breasts.

It wasn't enough, not nearly enough. As her pussy began to clench and spasm, it felt achingly empty. The desperate need made her moan and twist, wanting more, needing something thick and hard filling her.

Ty lifted his head and admired her nipples. They were red and sensitive from his constant attention. He watched her eyes darken to pure chocolate as Chase continued to rub the little bundle of nerve endings hidden between her thighs.

He could read her desire, understood her want. The little woman wanted to be fucked, but he did not intend to give in to her just yet. He wanted this to last, to suspend her in this moment of need and pleasure, to drive the sensations higher until there was nothing left but the three of them, hot, sweaty and clinging to each other.

Slowly, he began kissing and licking his way across her rounded stomach as he knelt before her. Taking his time, enjoying the journey, he worked his way toward the wet folds of her gleaming pussy.

"You greedy son of bitch," Chase muttered. "I wanted a taste of that."

Chase would have to wait. The sweet, musky scent of her desire drew him in and he wasn't about to stop. The pink, swollen folds temped him to rub his face against her softness, stroke his tongue over her creamy slit, devour her with long, hungry licks. Ty did not resist the temptation.

Tessa jumped when the tip of tongue slid up her pussy and brushed against her clit. He lapped repeatedly at the quivering button, working it into a firestorm of sensation. Chase was not about to be outdone. With an arm around her waist, he supported her as he bent his head to her breast and began tormenting her nipple in rhythm with the tongue buried between her pussy lips.

Her breath shortened to pants as her body shivered under the escalating pleasure. Then everything snapped and Tessa sobbed, bucking against them as mindless pleasure swamped her body. Her cries turned into a scream as Ty's tongue pierced the shuddering depths of her sheath, eating into her pulsing cunt with starved desperation.

Ty could not get enough of her. Spearing his tongue into the exquisite clench of her inner muscles, he fucked her with deep, greedy strokes until she flooded him with her lush, sweet cream.

A hard grip ripped him away from the sweet heaven he was enjoying. Ty growled, jerking his head free.

"Tough shit, buddy." Chase shouldered him out of the way. "It's my turn. Go hold her up."

Chapter 4

Tessa swayed with the loss of Chase's arm and was saved from falling to the floor when Ty stepped behind her, allowing her to melt into his solid strength. His words, given in such a rough voice, sent thrills through her. Here were two gorgeous men, fighting over who got to eat her pussy.

It was outrageous, beyond anything she had ever experienced and it sent a devilish flare of erotic euphoria through her. Everything about this moment was new. Normally shy and a little embarrassed by her body, she felt relaxed being naked, pressed between two men with their rough jeans rasping over her skin, the soft cotton of their T-shirts tickling. It heightened her sense of vulnerability, spicing her arousal with exotic flare.

Her body, already beginning to relax from the climaxes Ty forced on her, sparked to life again as Chase's mouth replaced the other man's. Large, work-roughened hands slid up her ribcage to palm her breasts as Ty's fingers curled around her hard nipples. They pulled and rolled the tender flesh, sending shards of pleasure radiating outward. Her head tipped backward. The movement arched her back, offering up her breasts for his caress.

Tessa's eyes rolled back in her head as pleasure bombarded every part of her body. Too much was coming at her too fast. She couldn't distinguish one caress from another as she drowned in a sea of rapture.

Chase ravished the swollen, weeping pussy before him, unable to quench his thirst. She was the most delicious thing he'd ever eaten. Her tight little pussy clamped down on his tongue, attempting to suck him in deeper as a flood of sweet cream gushed down.

Only one thing could be better than tasting Tessa's pussy, and that would be fucking it. His hardened flesh thumped at that thought, aching to be inside her now. Standing, he swept her up into his powerful arms. He needed to find someplace for them to get horizontal.

Tessa clutched at Chase's shoulders. She was lost in the onslaught of frenzied lust and was not sure where they were headed until she felt the softness of her mattress beneath her.

Ty followed the couple, ripping at his button and zipper. Not even taking the time to shove his jeans all the way down, he climbed on top of Tessa while Chase struggled out of his own clothes. Tessa didn't seem to mind the switch in partners.

Her legs parted easily, making a place for him between her soft thighs. Ty's heartbeat tripped over itself as she smiled up at him, her arms lifting to pull him closer. With an impatient motion, he hooked her legs over his elbows and embedded himself inside her with one hard thrust.

An inferno raged out of control inside him, one that flamed higher as he pounded into her tight, clenching depths. Her small sheath fought his invasion, conceding no more space than necessary. His lips pulled back in a carnal snarl as he forced her legs higher, wider, opening her for a deeper, harder penetration.

Tessa felt skewered on his thick, hard cock. Her heart was pounding too fast. She couldn't get enough air in as he thrust into her. Her hands fisted in the bed sheets as she fought not to drown in the tension gripping her.

She had never experienced pleasure such as this, was astonished to discover her body was capable of experiencing such rapture. When he shifted, reaching down to capture and manipulate her clit, the tension winding through her broke.

Every cell in her body exploded as great, rippling waves of ecstasy rocked through her in rhythm with the thick shaft slamming in and out of her clenching core. It was too much and Tessa twisted mindlessly within his grasp, trying to both escape and get closer.

Ty growled as he felt her convulse beneath him in orgasm. Her already tight inner muscles fisted around his cock, clamping him in a vise of sweet feminine heat. He could feel the white-hot pressure beginning to explode outward from his balls. Tipping his head, Ty roared out his release as he pumped himself furiously into her, dragging out the sensation to the last drop before he collapsed on top of Tessa.

Panting for breath, he did not try to make sense of what his body was feeling or the strange mix of emotions rolling through him. He simply accepted that had been the most satisfying experience he had ever endured.

He had been wild for her, completely obsessed with the pleasure she was giving him and he wasn't done. Not if his still-hard cock had anything to say about the matter.

Although he had just fucked her like a horny teenager with his first girl and survived a release that left his muscles weak and shaky, his cock was rock hard and ready to go another round. That hadn't happened to him since Chase and him were teens fooling around with Betty Anne in the backseat.

He felt her trembling beneath him a moment before the giggles began to trickle out of her. The lighthearted sound warmed him inside and he felt himself relax as he never did around women.

The glint of metal caught his eye and he tilted his head to study the circular ring clamped around her bedpost. He couldn't help but wonder if the delectable little minx beneath him had ever put them to use.

"You forgot to take off your pants," she teased, drawing his gaze back to hers.

"I'll try to do better next time."

"I'll do better this time," Chase said, and all but yanked Ty off Tessa.

Chase and Ty had shared many women during their long friendship, but this was the first time Ty had ever felt annoyed by Chase's participation. He wasn't jealous, but neither was he ready to give up the warm home his cock had found.

Chase really didn't care what Ty was feeling or thinking, all he wanted was to bury himself inside Tessa and take her for the ride of her life. She was smiling up at him with such joy and happiness that it gave him pause. He smiled back.

"Ready for the best, baby?"

"The best?" Tessa grinned, wrapping her arms around him. "Does that come with a money-back guarantee?"

"Mouthy little thing, aren't you?" Chase looked over at Ty, who was still scowling. "Think you can gag her with something so I can enjoy myself?"

"I might have something," Tessa heard Ty growl a moment before a hand slid into her hair, rolling her head to the side and the cock waiting for her. "It needs to be cleaned, darlin'."

Tessa's eyes widened at the size of his cock. It was bigger than she had imagined and explained why she had felt so full. She wasn't sure she could suck his entire cock into her mouth, but was willing to try.

With determined glint in her eyes, Tessa began to lick Ty's dick. The taste of their combined flavors was a potent mixture. With long, slow laps, she tasted his entire length, making him groan as his hips arched, pushing the bulbous head demandingly against her mouth. At the subtle prodding, she began to suck. The hand buried in her hair tightened as he pushed her head up and down along his length, teaching her the pace he liked.

Chase smiled. Tessa was one sensual woman. It was rare to find a woman who didn't feel the need to put up any maidenly protest or try too hard to be seductive. She just relaxed and enjoyed herself, seemingly unconcerned about anything.

Chase looked down the length of their bodies to where he was poised at her entrance. She was open, fully exposed, and he could see the combined juices of Ty's seed and her own cream seeped from her. Chase lifted her hips, aligning his cock to her dripping cunt. She whimpered as she felt him begin to press into her eager pussy.

"Am I hurting you?"

Tessa moaned, amazed that her body could so quickly accept another. Not just accept, but welcome. The aftershocks of her last climax were still tingling through her. They coiled with renewed tension, winding tighter as he forced inch after inch of his thick, hard erection deep into her.

Chase felt different, his strokes deep and slow, but no less arousing. Tighter and tighter, the tension wound through her muscles. Never breaking, the pleasurable ache pushed her higher and higher until she was sure that when it snapped her muscles would shred and there would be nothing of her left.

Chase's thrusts became hard, fast, demanding as he fucked into her clenching cunt. Ty matched Chase's enthusiasm, stroking his cock into her mouth with renewed speed. Everything blurred as her world exploded again.

Tessa's scream was caught in the back of her throat as the furious spasms ripped through her taut body. Pleasure crashed over her in mind numbing waves, taking her so far out of her body that her world crumpled.

She was vaguely aware of Chase's shout of fulfillment mingling with Ty's groan of release as they shot hot jets of semen into her. She swallowed, trying to take all Ty had to give before she slipped into oblivion.

Chapter 5

"Hey, sweetheart?"

Sweetheart?

Tessa's eyes popped open at the sound of an unfamiliar male voice. Whoever he was, he wasn't talking to her. His voice faded as he moved further across her apartment. For several tense moments, she lay still, trying to assimilate what was happening.

Memories of the past night played slowly through her mind. What the hell had she done? One-night stands with strangers weren't her thing, and sleeping with paid companions was definitely against her policy. But that wasn't the worst.

The worst was Ty was whispering; he obviously had a girlfriend and Tessa did not mess with other women's men. Her eyes closed as it occurred to her that maybe it were a boyfriend he was calling sweetheart.

Either way, the rule still stands. Where the hell is the other one?

Wherever Chase was, he wasn't in the bed. She listened carefully, but if he were still in the apartment, he was being exceptionally quiet. Hopefully, he was gone and that would just leave her with Ty to get rid of.

Tessa wanted to pull the covers over her head and hide. How was she supposed to face him? What was she supposed to say? If he were a lover, she'd smile and offer him breakfast, but that was unprofessional. Wasn't it?

She heard his footsteps returning and tensed.

Please, oh please, let him get dressed and leave. The sound of him collecting his clothes gave her hope, but then she heard the bathroom door shut. She was not out of hot water yet. Could she pretend to be asleep until he left? Would he just leave?

He'll probably wait to be paid. Tessa grimaced as that thought occurred to her. The agency would charge her credit card for services rendered, but she should probably tip him. What did one tip a prostitute? Was it the normal fifteen percent?

The man certainly earned a little extra. I haven't had that many orgasms since well, ever.

Okay, fifteen percent of fifteen hundred was two hundred and twenty-five, times two she didn't have that kind of money on her. She barely carried fifty dollars in her wallet. Maybe he'd take a check.

Petty cash. Tessa hopped out of bed and threw on her robe. Thankfully, only Marcie was in the office. Tessa barely paid her any mind as she went flying past, her bare legs peeking out of her robe. Marcie studied Tessa as she grabbed the petty cash box out from under her desk.

"Don't forget that Mrs. Ozora is showing up in half an hour." Marcie yelled at her fleeing back.

Whatever. Ozora was the least of Tessa's problems. Getting the red-hot rent-a-hunk out of her apartment was her main concern. It took her a moment to find her keys. Just as she pulled four hundred and fifty dollars from the small lockbox, she heard the bathroom door open.

Not giving Ty any time to say or do anything, she shoved the money into his hand.

"Thank you very much."

She grabbed him by the wrist and began dragging him through the apartment. She didn't let go till she'd gotten him to the door at the other side. It was the private entrance to her apartment.

"Tessa, I think we need to talk."

"You can tell the agency to bill me, that's a tip for Chase and you." She quickly undid the deadbolt and opened the door.

"But—"

"You provided excellent services, but I think we'll go with somebody else to handle Henry." She shoved him out onto the small landing.

"But—"

"Thank you for everything. Have a nice day."

Tessa slammed the door on him and collapsed against it. That had been one of the most embarrassing things she had ever done. The clock on her stove caught her eye and she blinked.

Oh, shit. Ozora!

* * * *

Ty stood staring in stunned shock at the metal door.
The fucking woman paid me!

He looked at the bills crumpling as his fist clenched around it.

Four hundred and fifty dollars?

He had been worth more than that and only half was his. Hell, he'd fucked her all night long, given her so many orgasms she'd passed out from the pleasure. He hadn't performed that well for a woman in decades and this is what he got?

Ty raised his fist, intending to beat the door down.

What the hell am I doing? This is all wrong.

His cock didn't care about the right or wrong of the situation. It had been hard since she had rushed him through the apartment. Her robe had parted to reveal the temptingly plump swells of her breast, the soft, sweet flesh of her inner tights, the delightful scent of her body...

Stop! God, just stop thinking about her like that.

That order didn't dent his cock's enthusiasm one bit, so Ty focused his thoughts on Olivia. His cock wilted and dropped, uninterested.

Since when did you get so picky?

Ty wasn't sure what this sudden fickleness meant, but he knew the answer wasn't going to come to him standing four stories in the air on an old wrought-iron landing. The only thing to do was retreat and plan.

Eight hours later, he still had no plan and his conscience had given him no break. He'd lied to Tessa and cheated on Olivia. Tessa. Her name stuck in his head as an image of her came to mind. His entire body tensed, his cock hardening and his heart picking up speed.

For the life of him, Ty could not understand his reaction to the wicked witch of South Bend. She was short, plump, rumpled. A far cry from the tall and tailored women he normally dated. Not at all like Olivia.

Olivia was intelligent, articulate, well-groomed and mannered and, above all, rational. So why was he standing here getting ready for his date with her with as much enthusiasm as a man about to attend a funeral?

"Hey." Chase knocked on his open office door. "What's with the tux?"

"Olivia's dad is throwing a fundraiser for some politician tonight." Ty turned to his friend.

"Hmm." Chase slumped into one of the big leather chairs that surrounded the small seating area in Ty's office.

"What are you up to tonight?"

"Going home to get a shower and then off to Tessa's."

Ty's mouth fell open. "Are you insane?"

"Most probably."

"Please tell me you haven't arranged this with her already."

"Nah, I was going to surprise her."

"Why?"

"Why not?"

"Before last night, you thought she was an evil bitch with a stick up her ass, or don't you remember that she's trying to stop our next development."

"I think I've figured a way around that."

"Really? What?"

"We wouldn't tear down the buildings, we'll build over them."

"Over them?"

"I've seen it done before. We'll incorporate them into our structure. We'll have to tear into some of them to make a central lobby, but then we can renovate them, make them into shops and stores."

Ty thought that over for a moment. It wasn't the worst idea.

"That sounds expensive," he commented begrudgingly.

"I'll have the architects look into it, see what they can figure out."

"We'll have to get new permits and agreements from the city."

"Not a problem."

"You never know what you're getting into with old buildings."

"Ty—"

"They could need to be completely gutted to bring them up to code."

"So, we—"

"Once you start tearing into them, who knows what you'll find."

"We'll—"

"We'll have to get new permits and approval by the city."

"You said that already."

"That will delay the project."

"Time is money." Chase rolled his eyes.

Ty nodded. "Exactly."

"But it will make Tessa happy." Chase held up his hands, raising one like a weight scale. "Tessa's happiness." His other hand dropped. "Money."

"Chase," Ty groaned. "You have to leave her alone."

"Why?"

"Because she thinks you're a whore. The woman frickin' tipped me this morning!"

"Really?" Chase grinned. "How much?"

"That's not the point!"

"How much?"

"Four hundred, I think."

"Hmm. I bet I can get more."

"It was to be divided between us," Ty snarled.

"Oh, well then, I definitely have to go back. Got a reputation to live up to."

"Chase." Ty took a deep breath. "You have to stay away."

"Sorry, man. I can't do that."

"Why not?"

"I like her."

"You like a lot of women."

"Not like this." Chase shook his head, becoming serious. "There is something about her, Ty. The sex last night, I've never…I just can't get her out of my mind."

"Get over it."

"Don't want to."

"What the hell do you think is going to happen here? You're going to try to make a relationship with a woman you have deceived from the start. How do you think she'll respond when she learns you're Chase Dunn from Banning & Dunn?"

"I imagine she'll go ballistic, do something completely irrational, but we'll work it out."

"Work it out." Ty repeated, amazed at his best friend. "You really are going to try and have a relationship with this woman."

"I have to." Chase stood. "The old hound dog has grown an inch longer than it ever has thanks to that little witch. She's got magical powers."

Chapter 6

The cheesy movie stopped bothering to progress its nonexistent plot and got down to the point: fucking. Eyeing the array of toys laid out on her coffee table, Tessa wondered how she had been reduced to this.

All day she had been horny, which was odd considering she had spent the entire night in the arms of the best lovers she had ever had. Okay, so they'd been paid lovers, which probably explained the multiple orgasms.

Nothing like the skill of an expert.

One would think that would have kept her happy for a while, but it had backfired, making her body crave even more pleasure. Problem was that the large collection of sex toys held little appeal compared to a real man. A man was what her body craved.

Two men, two very specific men. Tessa scrunched her lips and picked up one of the dildos.

Well, this is all I have tonight.

Most the toys were gifts from Marcie, that pervert. Marcie had pinned her against the wall and dragged the details of Tessa's torrid night with Ty and Chase out of her. Her friend had been appalled and excited all at once.

Tessa had taken Marcie's teasing, but when her friend had mentioned she might call the guys, Tessa had lashed back at her. The thought of Marcie with Ty and Chase made her sick, even though she knew she was being silly.

The men made their living off sex. That was the only reason they'd stayed the night. She was just a job to them. They were probably out right now working on another job.

She should just be thankful for the experience of a lifetime, even if it had cost her a bundle. At least she could afford it, thanks to the new order that had come in today. Mid-morning, some guy had e-mailed her company. He had identified himself only as Michael from somewhere in the Bahamas.

How he had ever heard of her, Tessa couldn't figure out, but that wasn't the strange part. He had explained that he was in love with the most beautiful woman. Apparently, his sweetheart tended to lose things, so he wanted not one, but two engagement rings made for her. No expense was to be spared and he was leaving the entire design up to them.

Tessa had written back that a down payment was needed to acquire the stones. That wasn't entirely the truth, but the e-mail had all the signs of being hoax.

She had been surprised when a courier arrived right before lunch with a cashier's check for five hundred thousand dollars. That was a lot more money than she had asked for, more money than she needed. A note with a few instructions was included with the check.

It was the strangest order she had ever received, but Tessa wasn't going to argue with a check that big. Not when she desperately needed the money. Her ongoing legal battle with Banning & Dun had taken out most of her savings.

Tessa scowled as her mind turned to those assholes, as she had labeled them after they had attempted to buy her out of the building. All the other tenants might have been willing to take cash, but Tessa's standards were higher. She wasn't going to settle for anything less than saving the beautiful, historic building from the destructive clutches of those barbarians.

While he was unconcerned about the ring design, her new client had some ideas about the box, which proved that rich people were strange. He didn't know the woman's ring size, so he had included her pant and shirt sizes. That just went to show he knew nothing about jewelry.

A knock at her back door cut off the silent tirade building in her head. Standing, she tightened the belt of her robe. She wasn't dressed for company, hadn't been expecting any.

Muting the guttural moans and cries coming from the TV, she picked up the cordless phone as she and inched into the kitchen doorway. The phone provided little protection, but it was the most she had. She'd programmed 911 into the speed dial years ago, just in case.

The banging came again, this time followed by a shout.

"Tessa!"

"Chase?" Tessa's eyes went wide, his name no more than a whisper. She cleared her throat and yelled, "Chase is that you?"

"Yeah, open up."

"Uh." Tessa's eyes darted around the living room. "Just a minute. Oh, Jesus," she muttered as she rushed around gathering the assortment of sex gadgets. The pounding came again along with Chase calling out her name. Feeling rushed, she shoved the armload of plastic vibrators and dildos into their plastic bin and kicked the container to the couch.

"Tessa!"

"I'm coming!"

She clicked off the TV and threw the remote onto the couch as she rushed for the door. Smoothing her hair, she took a deep breath before yanking open the door.

Chase greeted her with his Cheshire Cat grin. His eyes scanned down her robe, glad to see that she was already dressed for bed. His cock ignited at the idea of all that soft flesh concealed by her fluffy garment. All that stood in his way was a belt with a single, loose knot.

"Chase." Tessa clutched the sides of her robe together, as if he hadn't spent all last night caressing, kissing, learning every intimate curve of her body. "What are you doing here?"

"I brought a pizza." Chase held the large box up for her inspection.

"Pizza?"

"And beer." He pushed past her, sauntering into her kitchen and leaving her standing at the door with her mouth open.

"Beer?"

"Yeah, none of that sissy light stuff neither." Chase dropped the pizza and six-pack onto her table.

"What are you doing here?" She hastily closed the door and followed him.

"Dinner, duh."

Tessa's eyes widened as realization dawned. "You didn't come here for *that*, did you?"

"That?" Chase laughed. "In fact, I did come here for *that*."

"I don't think my bank account can afford this."

"Don't sweat it, baby." Chase pulled her into his arms. "We wouldn't tell the agency."

"I can't afford the tip either," Tessa muttered.

It was a half-hearted protest. She wasn't really planning on denying Chase. Already her body was softening, awakening with a desire that the porno had failed to inspire in her.

Chase slid his hands around her face and pulled her into his kiss, stopping only when their lips were barely touching to say, "This isn't for money."

Her lips were deliciously soft, temptingly sweet and he caught her sigh of contentment as he deepened the kiss. A strange feeling of satisfaction warmed him as she melted into him, responding and returning the kiss with equal passion.

The ache that had been bothering him all day finally disappeared as new ache grew in its place. The sudden change made him aware that as hard as his dick had been, the pain he had felt during the day had not been sexual frustration. It was something different, something more dangerous that was only assuaged by being near her. Chase didn't understand it, didn't want to investigate it. He'd rather accept the obvious and focus on the simpler pleasure of the flesh.

More roughly than he intended, he ripped off the belt of her robe and shoved his hands beneath the terrycloth, delighting at the soft flesh he discovered. He felt a tremor work its way through her body as his hand found her breast.

Tessa's heart fluttered and skipped a beat as Chase pulled back and she could see the hunger darkening his gray eyes. The way he looked at her was so sexy that she felt something strange and unfamiliar heat her insides. The emotion seasoned the desire pumping through her body, making it sharper, more potent.

His other hand slid into her damp pussy curls, drawing a whimper of need from her. His finger gently caressed the folds of her slit before sliding between the swollen lips. Unerringly, he found her sensitive button and began to tease the small, tender nub.

Chase bent his head to her breast, lapping and licking at her nipple in rhythm with his touch on her clit. He could feel her shuddering, twisting against him as the pleasure inside her mounted. Holding her close with his other arm, he increased the pressure of his fingers, the pace of his tongue on her breast.

Tessa feared that she was going to burst with the ecstasy slicing through her body. This was no slow climb, no seductive rise. He was driving her hard and fast straight up the mountain.

Her pussy throbbed and pulsed, grasping at the empty air as her orgasm broke over her, flooding her in a sea of pleasure. Her mouth fell open but her scream became trapped in her throat as her body bowed.

Chase held her through the devastating waves of her climax. His touch gentled, soothing now as he placed nibbling little kisses along her jaw line. He had never derived so much pleasure from just pleasing his partner.

"Well, that was a fine hello," Tessa teased as her breath began to even out.

"You should stick around for the second act."

"Really? That good huh?"

"It's a show-stopper."

"Then maybe you should stop talking and start showing." Tessa wrapped her arms around his neck and brought his mouth down to hers.

Chapter 7

Tessa's hands made quick work of Chase's shirt, desperate to feel his skin on hers. She murmured with delight when her fingers were finally touching his warm chest. The hard muscles pulling his skin smooth invited exploration.

Chase groaned as her fingers gently caressed their way down his torso before sweeping back up to tease his nipples. Empowered by the faint trembling she could feel shaking his body, Tessa became more aggressive. She pulled her mouth away from Chase's and began nibbling her way down his jaw and chest.

"What is so funny, pretty lady?" Chase growled, when he felt her smile against his skin.

"Nothing," Tessa whispered against his nipple before giving it a little lick. Chase growled at the quick touch. "Just thinking the second act belongs to the lady."

With that as a warning, her hand slid over the bulge in his jeans, slightly squeezing and measuring his erection. Chase arched his hips, his hand coming to cover hers, strengthening her hold.

"Oh, I agree," he murmured.

"Then let go of my hand." Tessa nibbled on his other nipple. "Or I won't be able to get it down your pants."

"Let me."

Chase made quick work of the row of buttons holding back his dick. Grabbing her hand, he didn't wait for her to move as he thrust himself into her palm. Tessa smothered a giggle at his impatience. Intentionally tormenting him, she refused to grab his hard length. Instead, she let her fingers gently slide down his cock, enjoying the heated, silky feel of his flesh. Chase groaned and jerked in her hold. Tessa smiled at his reaction to her touch.

Never before had she felt so powerful, so seductive as this man made her feel. Except maybe with Ty. That errant thought whispered through her brain, making her heart contract slightly.

Tessa shoved it away. She wasn't going to focus on who was missing, but enjoy the man who had showed up. It was a miracle that Chase was here. Men like him did not pursue women like her.

"God, baby." Chase groaned, drawing her attention back to the matter at hand and the soft balls she was now rolling gently between her fingertips.

Tessa grinned against his hot skin and began to kiss and lick her way down over his stomach, pausing to trace the firm lines of his abdomen with her tongue before continuing lower.

Chase held his breath as her mouth neared his straining cock. His balls were on fire and her gentle, teasing touches were driving him insane. He needed something more. Her hot mouth sucking on him was what he hoped for.

Then she was there, but he received no relief. Her tongue flicked out to delicately taste the white fluid leaking out of his unseeing eye. Chase jerked and cursed, his hand tangling in her hair and trying to urge her down on his cock.

Tessa resisted, continuing to torment him as she swirled her tongue around the broad head of his cock and down the sides. She rubbed her cheek against his hard length, delighting in the erotic contrast of hot silk stretched tightly over his rock-hard erection.

Slowly she explored him, learning all the ways he liked to be licked, where he was most sensitive, wanting to know how to please him. As she tormented his cock with her mouth, her fingers explored the soft sack at its base.

When her mouth joined her hands, gently tugging on his sensitive balls, Chase's heart beat a rapid tattoo against his chest. He growled, his hands pulling her away from his aching fresh.

"I can't take any more, baby." Chase rubbed the head of his cock against her lips. "Suck it."

He had given her so much pleasure last night. She wanted to do the same for him. Taking his shaft into her hands, she opened her mouth and slowly slid her lips down over as much of his cock as she could take.

Above her Chase groaned, a raw, guttural sound that fed her own excitement. With increasing speed, she sucked and pulled on his erection, his hands guiding her every motion. Soon the erotic sucking noises grew louder as his cock wept more and more fluid.

The blistering heat of her mouth, the tight suction of her cheeks, the velvety caresses of her tongue, everything she was doing was stripping away what little control Chase had. He wanted to savor the moment, to memorize every detail of having Tessa kneeling before him, servicing him, but it was too much.

The tightness in his balls was growing painful and he knew it was only seconds before her talented mouth ripped his seed from him. His hips thrust forward, trying to shove even more of his erection into her mouth, down her throat. She moaned, the sound vibrating against his flesh and snatching away his last restraint.

Blinding, white-hot pleasure seared him from his balls to his toes and up to his ears. His skin burned, shuddering with the explosive release as he flooded her mouth. Sweet little thing that she was, Tessa swallowed, taking everything he had to give her till there was no more.

She drained him of every drop, but couldn't deflate his erection. Despite his weak muscles and the threat from his heart to explode if forced to take another climax, his dick wanted more. That in itself was a testament to the power Tessa had over him.

Not that Chase was admitting he was old, but he had passed the point where he could come and keep on coming a few years back. He'd come to a point in his life where he needed a little break between sessions. At least, he had thought he had come to that point.

Last night Tessa had shown him it just took the right woman. Apparently it hadn't been a fluke, because he needed to be inside her now more than he had when had walked through her door. Chase lifted her, intending to carry her to the bed, but when he bumped into the couch, he figured that would do.

Toppling her back onto the cushions, Tessa felt the remote digging into her back. Unwilling to let him completely go, she used one hand to scrounge around for the remote. Finding it, she was pulling it out from under herself when his hand found her breast again.

Tessa gasped, her hand tightening reflexively over the remote and depressing the buttons. A second later, cheesy music filled the air along with the sensual sounds of moans and groans.

"What the...?" Chase's head turned to the TV.

"Shit." Tessa began pressing buttons at random, trying to find the off switch.

"What are you doing?"

Chase grabbed the remote and they fought over it. It popped out of their grasps and clanged onto the floor.

"You're watching porn."

"I'm an adult." Tessa could feel her face flame. "I'm allowed to watch porn."

"I didn't think women did that." Chase grinned down at her before turning back to the TV. "Look at that. That's kind of kinky."

"Oh, shut up." Tessa twisted, trying to reach for the remote. "You can't tell me that in your profession, you haven't ever done that."

"Don't assume anything," Chase murmured, fascinated by the bondage play going on in the movie.

"Where the hell did that remote go?" Her hand found the edge of the plastic container that hadn't made its way completely under the couch.

"I'll get it." Chase leaned over to reach down before she could stop him.

"No, wait!"

"What?" Chase frowned as his hand found something hard and plastic. Whatever it was, it wasn't a remote. "What is this?"

"Oh, God." Tessa cringed as she heard the scrape of the plastic container across the hardwood floor. She wished she could somehow magically disappear.

"Well, well, well." Chase chuckled. "This just gets more interesting."

"Oh, God."

"Porno and sex toys. It looks like my sweet, innocent little Tessa was planning one hell of a private party." She was a woman after his own heart. Not that he watched a lot of porn, but any woman willing to definitely got his respect.

"Oh, shut up."

"So tell me, sweetheart, after all the loving we gave you last night, why were you set to pleasure yourself tonight? Didn't we take good care of you?"

"No, it's not that. It's, well, you see…"

"Yes?"

"You're kind of like a chocolate chip cookie."

"Excuse me?" One of Chase's eyebrows rose. "I'm like a cookie?"

"Yeah. You eat one and it's really good, but it leaves you hungry for another."

"Or in this case, hungry for porn and vibrators, huh?"

"You can stop grinning at any time," Tessa muttered. "It's a perfectly healthy thing for a woman to do."

"But it's more fun with a partner."

"Really? Hmm, maybe I should call Marcie and see if she wants to join me."

"That's not what I was talking about." Chase lowered his head to her neck and began to nibble his way down the part in her robe.

Tessa sighed and ran her hands back into his hair. "Aren't you going to turn the TV off?"

"Let's see if we can keep time with the music."

Chapter 8

Ty didn't know what he was doing. He'd been at the party with Olivia, but his lack of attention had earned him a harsh rebuke. He'd excused his behavior with a lame, mumbled, "I don't feel well." It was partly the truth.

Ty did feel like shit, and felt worse around Olivia. He had weathered Olivia's sharp words and stormy eyes and left under the pretense of being sick. She had a right to be mad. She was going to be out of town on business for the next week and normally they expanded their farewells with a passionate evening.

He'd take her back to his playroom and they'd spend the night hot, sweaty and moaning. It was pretty wild stuff. At least it had seemed pretty wild, but now, with last night's memories of Tessa still warming his blood, Ty realized his definitions were changing.

That wasn't right. Comparing a one-night stand with Olivia made him feel more like a slug than he already did. Olivia was his girlfriend, damn near a fiancée. They had been going out for over a year, the longest he had ever been with a woman. She was perfect. Not just physically, but she was educated, cultured, ran her own multimillion-dollar company and enjoyed his version of kinky sex.

Well, minus Chase. Chase had never taken a shine to Olivia. The feeling was entirely mutual. Besides the fact that his best friend and girlfriend could barely tolerate each other, everything was perfect.

If everything is so perfect, why haven't you taken her home to meet the folks?

Ty sighed. He had been putting that one off. Olivia hadn't pressed. She probably thought it was because his background embarrassed him. That wasn't it. Not exactly.

He just couldn't envision Olivia on a pig farm. She knew about his family back in Alabama, but knowing and smelling were two very different things. Olivia had too much class and manners to intentionally insult his family, but that didn't mean it wouldn't happen.

He could only imagine how hurt his mother would be if Olivia declined to eat the large homemade meals she loved to produce for company and there was no way Olivia would eat it. Everything was made with fatback, lard and butter, the vegetables were cooked till they were soggy, and then there was the meat. Olivia, with her strict vegetarian diet, would probably go into shock if she tried to eat his mom's cooking.

Tessa would probably gorge herself.

Unwanted, the image of Tessa and his mom working together in the kitchen came to mind. Tessa would charm his parents. There was no doubt in his mind about that. She had the same type of insane charm that Chase had, and they adored him.

As Ty thought about it, he realized that Chase and Tessa did have a lot in common. Both devised crazy, convoluted solutions to relatively simple problems. Both steamrolled over people, but with a smile and a wink they managed to endear themselves to their victims. Both tended to laugh during sex, giving in to their passionate nature with carefree abandon when so many people were intensely cautious of making a mistake.

Ty included himself in the latter group. Oh, he enjoyed sex and had more escapades than most men dreamed of, but there was a part of him that had always held back. Sex was just a physical exercise, an enjoyment of the flesh.

Ty had never allowed himself to become emotionally involved. That way lay danger and he had watched too many friends suffer the pitfalls of jealousy, anger, pain, marriages, divorces, depressions. No, that was not going to be his fate.

That was exactly why Olivia was the perfect choice. They enjoyed a passionate physical relationship, sure, but their life together wasn't based on it. No, their relationship was solidly rooted in mutual respect, common goals and aspirations. They agreed on everything from decorating styles and investment strategies to how to raise children.

So what if he didn't look forward to seeing her with bated breath. If she didn't make his heart pound and his head feel light. If she didn't inspire his cock to stay hard for five hours straight.

At least Olivia didn't drive him insane with ass-backward schemes that were destined to blow up in her face. Nor did she babble on, completely ignoring what he was saying until he had to kiss her just to get her attention.

Ty parked his truck and looked up at the old building. He hadn't meant to end up here. This was the last place he should be. It must be his conscience, it had brought him back here to do the right thing.

That's what he was going to do. It was time to tell Tessa the truth. He mounted the wrought-iron steps with a determined stride, his stomach tightening as he imagined all her possible reactions. This was not going to go well, but he wasn't going to chicken out.

He had raised his hand to knock on her door when a scream echoed out of the apartment. His heart seized as the sound repeated itself. Images of Tessa being hurt, beaten, possibly even raped seared through his mind.

This was not the safest neighborhood and she was pretty much alone in it. There were all sorts of deviants out there who would look at woman like Tessa and see her as a desirable and easy mark. Whoever was attacking Tessa now, Ty would kill him.

By the time she screamed for a third time, he had slammed through the door. Roaring Tessa's name, he raced through the kitchen and came to a sudden stop in the entrance to the living room. His eyes widened as he took in the scene before him.

Chase was sitting on the couch and Tessa was straddling him, shuddering in the obvious throes of a climax, her body sweaty, her eyes glassy, her large breasts swollen and flushed while Chase watched him rush in with a smug smile.

Chase might have been aware of Ty's dramatic entrance, but Tessa was obviously too overwhelmed to have noticed. An array of sex toys was strewn over the coffee table. Some cheap porn movie was playing on the TV, the classic tone of fuck-me music blaring through the room. It took Ty's befuddled brain a moment to process it all.

Tessa heaved a big sigh and collapsed on top of Chase, drawing Ty's eyes back to the couple. That same strange feeling passed through Ty. This time, he knew what it was: envy. He wanted to be the man she had just ridden to obvious exhaustion.

"Well, well, well. Look who showed up to the party late."

"I don't think he dressed for beer, pizza and porn," Tessa mumbled.

"Still got some sass left in you, huh, baby?" Chase slapped her ass, making Tessa stiffen and gasp. "How about we let Ty take the dildo out of your ass and slide his dick in? Then we'll see what you have to say."

Chase's words had an instant effect on Ty's cock. Already hard due to the erotic scene before him, it thickened, pushing painfully against the zipper confining it. He liked the sound of what Chase was proposing.

"Hmm." Tessa gave him a sleepy, seductive smile over Chase's shoulder as she eyed his obvious erection. "He certainly does look up for the task."

"You like the look of that, huh?" Chase cast a quick glance at Ty before turning back to Tessa. "You want that buried in your ass? You want to be stuffed full of cock?"

"Only if it's eight inches or longer."

Tessa's shriek of mock outrage almost drowned out the crack of Chase's hand coming down on her ass a second time.

"You're just too mouthy for your own good, you know that girl?"

Ty could see Chase's arm moving back and forth behind her, knew that he was fucking the dildo in and out of her ass. The slow, even slides were making Tessa moan and twist. Her whole body was shivering as she bit into her bottom lip.

God, she was beautiful. Her wild honey curls framed her sweet face. Her hazel eyes had darkened nearly to black with desire. Her breast were flushed, her pink nipples puckered with her desire.

Whatever good intentions or internal struggles had brought him here were forgotten as he watched her slowly climb toward another climax. His cock was raging to be set free, to be the one buried deep inside her, pounding her into release.

"That's what you want, isn't it, baby?" Chase was nibbling on Tessa's neck, teasing her. "You want to feel a real cock pumping into your beautiful behind. You want us both fucking into you at the same time. Him in your ass, me in your pussy."

"I think you've had enough pussy," Ty stated as he moved forward, his hands going to the front of his pants to free his erection. Without warning, he lifted Tessa straight off Chase's lap. Chase's cock popped out of Tessa's sheath with a sucking noise, telling Ty just how wet and ready she was.

"Hey! I was comfortable, you know."

"Tough shit." Ty wrapped Tessa's legs around his own waist and, with a single hard thrust, buried himself to the hilt in her warm, welcoming cunt. Tessa's head dropped back, her eyes closing as her entire body bowed into his.

Ty smiled and began walking to the bedroom, the motion teasing his little woman. He didn't bother to look at Chase as he spoke.

"Get the door, Romeo. I've got the woman."

Chapter 9

Tessa bit her lip. Her vision wavered as her eyes watered, threatening to spill tears, of joy or pain, she wasn't sure. The two emotions swirled together in a confusing mess as the thick head of Chase's cock popped through the tight fist of muscles at the entrance of her ass.

His cock was a lot bigger, thicker than the dildo they had used on her the night before. Ty was murmuring incoherent phrases as he kissed away her tears. Despite his attempt to comfort her, he was part of the problem. His massive erection was already fully buried inside her pussy, stretching her tight sheath to capacity and leaving little room for Chase as he attempted to forge his way into her back channel.

She'd been too exhausted last night to get to this. Ty had ridden her with an insatiable need through three climaxes before giving in to his own. He'd been like a man possessed, trying to outrace something he didn't want to deal with.

As Tessa had drifted off to sleep, she'd thought about how different Chase and Ty were. Chase made her feel like a teenager again, flushed and giddy with excitement. Ty, on the other hand, made her feel like a seductress.

A sexy, dangerous woman that provoked an animalistic lust in him that he was incapable of controlling. Between her two new lovers, she had never felt so confident and desirable. They made her feel loved. Wrapped in that warm emotion, she had fallen into a peaceful slumber.

She'd awakened hot and horny. She thought an erotic dream was the source of the wetness between her thighs, but it was her men. Tessa had opened her eyes and found herself tied to the bed on all fours.

Ty and Chase had treated her to a deluxe round of orgasms in the last hour. Alternately they had buried their heads between her legs and used their tongues, lips, fingers to drive her mercilessly to climax after climax.

While she'd been a puddle of jelly, panting for breath, her mind still trying to reboot, they'd stealthily lubed up her ass. Before she could form a complaint, Ty had slid beneath her, sheathing himself to the hilt in her weeping pussy.

Now it was Chase's turn. The pain blurred with the pleasure still rippling through her body, combining into a pointed mix of sensation. The sharp pull of muscles stretching sent fine prickles of pain up her spine. The small stings were dampened by the pleasured fullness of having both her pussy and ass filled by long, hard cocks.

"Oh, God." Chase's head dropped to her shoulder.

The small motion settled him more deeply into her tight, channel. The sensation sparked a wildfire of pained pleasure that threatened to consume her and she groaned with the sensation.

"It's okay, baby." Ty kissed her. "We're going to make you feel all right."

"Ty. I don't—"

She wasn't sure if she were objecting or encouraging. It didn't matter. The words were lost in her gasp as Chase reached around to trap her clit between his thumb and forefinger. Tessa moaned, begging him incoherently not to.

Her clit was a swollen, torturous knot of lust. Sharp spikes of pleasure so intense it was almost painful radiated through her as he began to rub the little bud. It was too much. Her already over-stimulated pussy couldn't take any more. It bit down hard on the cock buried there, contracting her butt muscles to squeeze the other cock lodged inside her.

Tessa screamed as Ty trapped one of her nipples with his teeth and began matching Chase's rolling rhythm with her clit. Her body convulsed as it exploded with another climax.

This one was unending as Ty began to move, prolonging her pleasure. Each stroke made her feel overfilled, stretched beyond her limits, as he pushed her against Chase's cock. It was an exquisite torture. One she was sure was going to kill her.

Then Chase started to move. The pressure from her ass abated for a second, only to become more extreme as he forged his way back through the tight fist of her muscles. Tessa clenched her teeth, holding back another scream as sharp explosions of pain detonated into a rain of intense rapture.

They took possession of her body with slow, easy strokes, but soon that consideration was washed away in a tide of desire. Their speed picked up, plunging harder, faster till her pussy was sizzling with pleasure, her ass burning with fire. Reality ceased to exist, thinned down only to the feel of the twin steel-hard cocks fucking into her with vicious ferocity. Her hips flexed, matching them stroke for stroke.

Chase ground his teeth together, trying to hold back his release until Tessa found hers. It was the hardest thing he had ever done, with her sweet ass gripping his cock in its velvet vise. It was the most amazing sensation he had ever experienced.

He felt Tessa explode beneath him. Her ass tightened down on his cock as shudders raced through her body. He gripped her hips hard, holding on as she bucked wildly beneath him and cried out with her pleasure.

Tessa screamed as her body splintered into a million tiny fireballs and still Ty and Chase continued to fuck her with hard, savage strokes. The small shards of piercing flames collapsed into each other, growing into a bonfire of delight as her body began to tense, anticipating the second, more powerful, explosion to come.

When she could climb no higher, she tumbled into the fiery labyrinth. Lost in a world defined only by searing ecstasy, she collapsed into sobs. Her two lovers joined her in the bliss of ecstasy a moment later and Tessa felt herself being flooded with the proof of their releases.

Chase fell over onto his side with a massive sigh, leaving Tessa collapsed on top of Ty. Now that was the way to start the day. The only thing better would be to spend the rest of the day repeating the morning's pleasantries.

He could call in sick to work. What did he have to do today? Go to a meeting with the architects to go over the new plans for South Bend.

Shit!

Chase checked his watch. He was going to be late. He jarred Tessa when he jumped out of bed, earning him a grumpy, murmured protest.

"Sorry to fuck and run, baby, but I got a meeting to make." Chase dropped a quick kiss on Tessa's head. She didn't bother to look up, just made another grumpy noise and waved him away.

After a quick shower, he shrugged into his clothes. It wasn't his normal business suit, but everybody who worked with him knew that some days he came into work in jeans. That was how it was sometimes.

Stepping back out into Tessa's bedroom, he was surprised to see Ty still in bed. He would have thought that Ty would be rushing off to nurse his guilty conscience and come up with all sorts of reasons for why he regretted the past night.

At the moment, Ty didn't look like he was regretting much of anything. He had one arm wrapped around Tessa, his other hand holding hers trapped against his chest. Ty may protest and fight all he wanted, but Chase could see the obvious. Ty was falling for Tessa the same as he was.

Chase didn't make a sound as he slipped out of the apartment, leaving the two lovers to sleep it off.

Ty listened to his best friend leave. Despite what Chase thought, he wasn't sleeping. His eyes were closed and his body relaxed, but he wasn't about to fall asleep and miss out on getting to hold Tessa close.

He didn't let himself think about the right or wrong of his actions, whether or not there was a future for them, nothing that would threaten the contentment making him feel better than he ever had.

Even when the idea that he would be happy to spend the rest of his days just like this, cuddled up close to Tessa, circulated through his mind, he didn't let it bother him. For once in his life, he simply accepted the truth and didn't bother to analyze it or fight it. He simply accepted that this felt right.

Chapter 10

"Go straight to jail. Do not pass go. Do not collect two hundred dollars."

Tessa laughed with glee as Ty read the card in his normal somber tone. She had learned over the week that her lovers took games very seriously. It was very different from the way she played.

Tessa had mastered Monopoly, Clue, Scrabble, even Chess as a child thanks to her parents' avid fascination with playing games. In college, she had continued her education and received a minor in cards. Everything from Spades to Hearts to Bridge, she and Marcie had wasted many nights playing cards.

They still had their college Rummy count sheet. To this day, they added to it. It was their lifetime goal to see how high they could get. When one died, the other would finally know who had won the game.

"You think that's funny, huh?" Ty dropped the thimble into jail. "Wait till you land on Pacific Avenue, baby. Then we'll see who is laughing."

Tessa grinned and looked over the board. It was covered in little red hotels, mostly on Ty and Chase's property. They were both masters at Monopoly.

"Look at the board." Tessa shook her head. "You two should have been developers."

Tessa surveyed the piles of fake money each man had, not noticing the way they tensed at her comments. Looking down at her own sparse lump of bills, Tessa shook her head. She'd be lucky to make it around the board without losing any clothing.

It was a common outcome when they played Monopoly, which was exactly why Chase had selected this game. Every night for the past week, they had come over and played one game or another.

Chase had suggested that they make things interesting by offering the winner a reward. In his horny and perverted mind, the best reward was a sexual one. When it came to Monopoly, Chase and Ty had no qualms about asking Tessa to prostitute herself for a loan or a pass over their properties.

Not that Tessa minded. The longer she stayed in the game, the deeper in debt she became to them, and the better the after-game entertainment would be.

It had started with relatively normal things, nudity, blowjobs, sexual positions, nothing too progressive or kinky. Chase had been the first to up the ante by having her put on a little show for them. Tessa had followed suit by requesting that they make a homemade porn film.

Neither man had minded fulfilling her desire. Ty in particular had seemed to revel in her willingness to try new things, and the other night after he had won a game of Trivia Pursuit, he raised the bar even higher.

He'd tied her wrists to the bed and then pulled out a toy he'd brought over. Tessa's eyes had widened as he'd run the velvety straps of the flogger teasingly over her body. When he'd said he was going to do whatever he wanted to her, that was not what she had in mind.

She'd watched the flogger with an anxiety made worse by the dark look in Ty's eyes. The only one who had been openly eager and excited by what was about to happen was Chase. He had moved the chair from beside her closet door to the foot of the bed, a front row seat for the show.

The first hit had taken Tessa by surprise. The light blow to her nipples had sent sparkles of tingly pleasure cascading through her body. She'd relaxed, thinking she could easily handle it, but soon the gentle blows grew harder. The teasing pleasure bloomed into intense rapture as Ty whipped her breasts, stomach, thighs and, finally, pussy, sending her from one climax into another.

"Ah, that sweet ass is mine now, baby." Chase chuckled as Tessa pushed her racecar onto Park Place.

Tessa heaved a dramatic sigh. "How much?"

"I'll let you pass and collect later."

"A deferred payment?" Tessa didn't buy Chase's nonchalant look any more than she did his sudden generosity.

"You could look at it that way."

"What's the interest rate?"

"So suspicious." Chase shook his head sadly. "What have I ever done to earn such distrust?"

"I know you, Chase. You're a dirty old man in the making." Tessa tried to keep her tone disapproving.

"I'm trying, baby." Chase grinned at her and then laughed. God, she was cute when she narrowed her eyes on him, her lips pursing with thoughtful distrust. It almost made him want to give up his plans and start demanding the clothing off her back.

She would give that to him, as she had in the past several days as they managed to pervert almost every game into a strip version. Tessa normally ended up naked by the time the game was over.

The idea thrilled Chase. There was nothing more beautiful than a naked Tessa, except maybe a climaxing Tessa. Or when she was pleasuring herself. Or when she had her lips spread wide, about to suck on his cock. Hell, he liked Tessa any way he could get her. It amazed him how looking at her, just being near her, made him feel relaxed, at peace. Chase shook his head at his thoughts.

He had become one of *them*. A man in love, mooning over his girl. Their girl, Chase corrected himself as his eyes cut over to Ty. Ty hadn't said anything, but Chase knew what he was feeling. It was there on his face for even the blind to see.

So was the fact that Ty was fighting it with everything he had. Oh, he couldn't manage it when she was around, but when they were at work everybody could tell he was wound up about something. Their employees all thought it was the industrial development currently under construction, but Chase knew better.

Ty had a free pass this week with Olivia away on a business trip, but she'd be back tomorrow and Ty was going to have to make his decision. That was what was weighing his friend down.

Ty thought he needed a woman like Olivia. It didn't matter to him if he loved her. She was part of his plan. What made Ty the best business partner Chase could ever have asked for was the same thing that made him a royal pain in the ass sometimes.

Ty believed in plans, well-structured, rational plans that guided his every motion. It was part of his organized, orderly way of handling life. That was fine, to a point. That point was Tessa, as far as Chase was concerned.

Tonight was the last night they had to spend completely unconcerned before Olivia got back. Chase wanted to make it memorable, to try and swing the pendulum as far in Tessa's favor as possible. Even if he failed, it would be one hell of a memory. With that thought in mind, Chase decided there was no point in wasting time playing a game.

"What are you—?"

"Come on. Ty why don't you put up the game." Chase suggested as he lifted Tessa out of her seat and started to move her to the bedroom. Tessa didn't offer any resistance, despite her obvious hesitation.

"Chase!" Tessa laughed as he muscled her into the bedroom. "We haven't even finished playing."

"Yeah, well, you lost." Chase shrugged. "Now it's time to pay up, sweetheart."

"I haven't lost." Tessa watched as Chase threw open her closet door and started rifling through her clothes. "Not yet."

"You bankrupted on Park Place."

"Ty might loan me the money." Tessa sighed at the amused look Chase tossed her over his shoulder. "Okay, so what is it tonight?"

"Dessert." Chase turned with one of her sundresses in hand. "Get dressed."

"I am dressed." Tessa was really confused. Normally they asked her take off her clothes, not put them on. This change left her more than a little suspicious. Chase was definitely up to something, but she didn't have a clue about what he was planning.

"I like this dress. I won the game, so put it on and get yourself ready to go out," Chase commanded, tossing the dress onto her bed.

"We're going out?" Tessa followed Chase to the bedroom door. "Wait! What are you planning?"

"Like I said, dessert." Chase didn't even bother to look back at her. "Now get dressed."

Tessa looked at the sundress. Something was definitely up. The only way to find out the details was to go along for the ride.

Chapter 11

Tessa frowned at Chase's big Dooley. It was definitely a macho man's truck. Black with lots of chrome, it was jacked up slightly to accommodate the oversized tires with their flashy rims. The blackout-tinted windows hid a luxurious interior.

This was the first time she was seeing anything they owned and it kind of shocked her. The vehicle had to cost a bundle, well over thirty thousand. That seemed a lot for a construction worker, but Tessa guessed he had either saved his money or was in debt up to his tight ass.

Chase lifted her onto the leather-upholstered bench seat when she hesitated. Tessa was still confused by what was happening. She'd thought she'd figured it out after Chase walked out of the bedroom. She'd removed her bra, donned her sexiest pair of panties and gotten ready to be asked to give them a strip tease.

It had totally shocked her when Chase and Ty led her out of the apartment. Apparently, dessert tonight really meant food. Chase explained that they wanted to check out this new late-night dessert bar. It was a concept Tessa hadn't even known existed, but apparently the place served high-end sweets with after-dinner drinks.

That was another surprise. Tessa hadn't thought of them as being cocktail kind of guys. In her mind, she had assumed that they were an old wooden bar, with an Irish name and dartboard, kind of men. It highlighted how little she knew about them.

Over the past week, she had thought she had come to know them pretty well. It was disconcerting to realize everything she knew about them was only what they had told her. They could have hidden lives, ones that were completely separate from her.

That sounded a little dramatic, but the doubt was seeded. They had spent so much time talking and getting to know each other that it hadn't really dawned on Tessa that they never left the apartment. She'd been too busy enjoying herself.

They had talked about everything. Ty had even insisted on looking through her portfolio of jewelry designs. Tessa had sat tensely as both men examined the extensive collection of photographs. Every time she made a piece, Marcie had taken a picture of it to add to the portfolio.

Unlike many jewelers, who only kept books displaying their finest pieces, all Tessa's work had been immortalized. Everything from her disasters to her greatest achievements was on display for them.

It had been nerve-wracking for her. Her mind told her not to worry. If Ty and Chase didn't like her stuff, what did that really mean? They worked construction, what did they know about jewelry?

Still, she couldn't overcome the need for their approval. When they had given it, she had blushed and floundered in embarrassment at their praise. It was the best feeling, even better than when she had won carious prizes for the more creative designs that she had shown at a variety of show.

She had reciprocated the interest. They'd confirmed her suspicion that they worked construction. Apparently escorting was just something they had accidentally fallen into on the side. It wasn't something they did on a regular basis as far as she could tell.

Not that they had volunteered a lot of information about their job. When she'd tried to find out more about what they did for a living, they had shrugged off most her questions. Ty had looked uneasy and Chase had quickly changed the conversation. Tessa had shrugged off the incident. They probably didn't think she'd be interested in talking about construction and it was definitely not good manners to talk about other women, especially when they had dated them for money.

Besides, there were plenty of other things to talk about. They were more than willing to share stories about their childhood, their families, their interests and hobbies. Ty's favorite subject was history. Not surprisingly, Chase's was sports. Tessa didn't know much about football or baseball, but she could hold her own when it came to academic subjects.

Suddenly now, after a week, she felt like she was going on her first date with them as they slid onto the bench seat, tucking her neatly between them as had become their habit. She cast a quick glance into the backseat.

"Two bench seats?" Tessa turned her eyes back to Chase as he started the engine. "Isn't that odd?"

"Custom made." Chase pushed the gearshift into drive and shot her a quick smile. "I like to be comfortable."

Tessa didn't have to wonder about that comment and didn't want to hear anymore. The idea of Chase with another woman was enough to make her ears go red and her heart to clench painfully. It didn't matter if it had been in the past.

"That's why he got an automatic," Ty chimed in. The hand he had resting on her leg began to rub circles on the inside of her knee. It was a distracting caress and she just blinked back at him, trying to process what he had said.

"An automatic?"

"Ty thinks it's girlie," Chase said.

Ty snorted. "Real men only drive sticks."

"I thought it was women who drove sticks and men just owned them." Tessa managed to get that line out as Ty's hand moved further up her leg, pushing the hem of her dress out of his way.

"Just can't control that sassy mouth, can you?" Chase dropped a hand onto her other leg. "I guess we're going to have to give you something else to think about than making sharp comments."

Tessa didn't have to guess at what he was going to give her, or how this planned outing was going to go. Their hands sliding up her thighs told her all she needed to know. They were going to torment her, then make her sit through dessert with wet panties and an aching pussy.

Well, no, thank you.

Tessa clamped her legs tightly together, inadvertently trapping their hands. Her attempt at stopping them backfired as rough fingertips drew teasing designs against her sensitive skin. Their touch tickled and began to ignite a slow burn up her legs to fire up her cunt. She squirmed, trying to douse the flames before they became any hotter.

"That's cute, Tessa." Chase laughed. "But you know better than to deny us."

Yes, she did and she wasn't surprised when Ty's other hand came to manually separate her thighs. Over the past few days, she had learned that resistance only seemed to rile Ty to greater heights of barbaric behavior. When his more savage, dominant side presented itself, Tessa always responded by melting, her own desire feeding off his need to master her.

Which is why when he lifted her leg over his own, spreading her wide right there on the bench seat, her pussy clenched and gushed. Ty kept his hand on her knee, pinning it in place and leaving her completely vulnerable to Chase and him.

"Panties." Chase tsked as his fingers discovered the last remaining barrier keeping him from her pussy.

Tessa knew what was coming next, but nevertheless cringed as Ty ripped her underwear away from her body. She didn't have time to lament the destruction of her nicest pair of panties as their fingers immediately began to tease her pussy. Chase took her clit, teasing her little bud with flicks and swirls that sent pleasure streaking through out her body. Ty slid two fingers between the wet folds of her sex, easily sliding them into her weeping cunt.

Tessa cried out at the intrusion, but her cries quickly turned to moans as her hips flexed, trying to match the rhythm of the thick digits fucking into her. It felt wonderful, the flames searing her pussy crackling higher, igniting an inferno that quickly threatened to consume her.

They pushed her closer and closer to climax, but it didn't hit till Ty nuzzled the top of her sundress down to reveal one swollen breast. His lips immediately latched onto her engorged nipple and sent waves of pure heat crashing over her, through her as her muscles contracted harshly and her pussy spasmed out of control.

With their usual relentlessness, they did not stop, but pushed her through one climax and into another. By the time Chase parked the truck, Tessa was sobbing, begging to be taken back to her place.

She promised them anything they wanted, rambling out all sorts of tempting ideas. She realized her efforts were futile when Ty lifted his head, his wet hand coming up smooth her dress back into place.

"Sorry, sweetheart." Chase killed the engine. "The fun is just beginning."

"Fun?" Tessa blinked, trying to regain her focus. There was a brick wall in front of them and as she turned her head she could see that they were parked between two buildings. Neon signs indicated one was open for business.

She pulled herself up, trying to close her legs and prepare to get out of the vehicle.

"Not yet, baby." Ty held tight to her one leg, keeping her spread.

"What are you—?" Tessa's eyes went wide as she felt Chase slide something smooth and cold into her pussy. "Chase!"

"Now you're ready." Ty lowered her leg back to the seat. He caught her hands when she moved to pull out whatever Chase had pushed into her.

"What did you—?" This time Tessa's question ended in a shriek as the little ball inside her started to vibrate.

"You better not do that when we get inside," Ty murmured in her ear before nibbling lightly on her lobe. "You don't want everybody to know what's going on."

"You...you can't..." Tessa couldn't get the words out. Her body was on the verge of peaking, every muscle tightening for the coming explosion as pleasure took control of her.

"Yes, we can," Chase said a moment before the vibrations stopped. Tessa collapsed against the seat, heaving and moaning slightly. As embarrassing as it would be to climax in a public parking lot, she needed that release.

The sound of Ty shoving open the truck door had her head rolling in his direction.

"We just did." With those final words, Ty latched onto her arm and pulled her unresisting body out of the truck.

Chapter 12

It was hell. For over a half an hour, Ty and Chase chatted, drinking beer and eating chocolate cake. Tessa said nothing, too afraid of what sounds might come out if she opened her mouth. Instead, she clenched her jaw and sat there panting through her teeth with her knees closed for fear of what would happen if she parted them.

Chase was using a remote to click the damned vibrating egg on and off, playing dictator while he tormented her at his leisure. This experience was nothing compared to what they had put her through the past few days. Knowing that they were in public should have dampened her enthusiasm.

It should have, but it didn't.

Her body was primed and ready, mental images of them shoving her onto the table and fucking her right there in the middle of the crowded dessert bar made her pussy clench and pulse with need. The idea of the other customers watching only made her shiver with arousal, not unlike when they had made their little film.

Tessa bit down on her lip as Chase clicked the egg back on and her pussy lit up. The vibrations echoing out of her cunt were magnified, making her quiver with the first shudders of release.

The taste of a metallic, coppery liquid hit her tongue and she realized she had bitten her lip. Chase frowned at her, his eyes tracking the thin flow of blood. Gently, he wiped it away, clicking the vibrating egg off.

"I guess it's time to go."

Tessa wasn't capable of responding. She watched with wide, glassy eyes as Ty threw some bills down on the table and offered her a hand. Tessa was terrified to get up. She was so wet she feared the little egg would slip out of her once she stood.

There was no hope for it and she let Ty wrap a supporting arm around her as he escorted her out of the building. She was grateful for the low lights, sure that she had left wet spot on the back of her dress.

When they turned the corner into the parking lot, Chase pressed himself into her side, lending her even more support.

"Poor baby," Chase murmured, his hot breath stirring her hair and tickling the shell of her ear. "You need a cock, don't you?"

Numbly, Tessa nodded. It was the truth. She needed to be fucked, and she needed it badly.

"Don't worry." They brought her to a stop beside the truck. "I'll take care of you in just a minute."

She thought he was referring to how long it would take them to get home, but when the truck's alarm system beeped and he opened the back door, it dawned on her he really did mean a minute.

She didn't offer any protest or resistance when he lifted her onto the backseat and climbed in behind her. She paid Ty no attention as he slid into the front seat, too focused on Chase, who was already shoving her dress up and out of the way.

Their hands bumped, colliding as she tore at his button-flies and he fished the egg out of her pussy. Before Ty had even started the truck, Chase's hands were cupping her butt cheeks and angling her up for his invasion.

Leaning down, he sealed their lips together. With one hard plunge, he embedded himself to the hilt in her softness. He swallowed her cry and gave in to the primitive need taking control of him. Never breaking rhythm, he ripped at the front of her dress, wanting to watch her breasts bounce as he fucked her.

She wasn't going to last. He body was over-primed and the knowledge that only the tinted windows separated them from the eyes of the pedestrians and other vehicles nearby made the experience hotter, more erotic. After only four strokes, Tessa came in a blinding flash of white-hot rapture. Then her body was flying in a million directions, no longer bound to the real world. She forgot everything, forgot they were in a truck driving through the busy downtown streets, focused only on the steel pole driving into her harder and deeper with every stroke.

Chase was not done, far from it. Nothing felt as good as pumping himself in and out of her tight sheath. He held back his release, trying to make the experience last as long as he humanly could. He rode her all the way home, driving her through three consecutive climaxes before giving in to his own. Tessa was barely aware of him collapsing onto top of her. His heavy weight meant nothing. She was still swimming through a sea of ecstasy.

When the truck door opened, the fresh air was held back by the musky, heavy scent of sex. The air felt cold against her overheated skin, making goose bumps break out all over her body. It was annoying and her irritation grew when Chase shifted, lifting off her and exposing more of her body to the cool breeze. She didn't want to move, didn't want anything to puncture the moment. All she wanted to do was curl up with her lover and fall asleep. That was not to be. As Chase sat up, Ty began to pull her out of the truck.

Tessa blinked open her eyes as she ended up in Ty's arms. She fully expected him to carry her up to her apartment. When he set her on the ground, forcing her feet to hold her own weight, she was caught off guard and almost fell. Her knees buckled, her legs unable to perform their function. Ty's arm circled her waist, holding her steady and earning him a shaky smile. The thin sundress was skewed, her breasts still hanging out over the top.

She became increasingly aware that she was now standing on a public sidewalk. Her hands went to the top of her dress and she began to pull it up over her breasts. When Ty reached for the hem, she thought he was going to help straighten her clothing. It caught her completely by surprise when he whipped the dress straight up and off.

Before she had time to gasp in surprise, much less process the fact that she was now only wearing a pair of heels, his tongue was invading her mouth. Cupping her butt cheeks, he lifted her. Instinctively, her legs wrapped around Ty's waist, her ankles hooking to keep her from falling.

The rough cut of his jeans biting into her thighs and the feel of his engorged cock rubbing against her satiated cunt warned her that he already had his pants open, had opened them before he even pulled her out of the truck.

He staggered forward until her back was pressed against the uneven molding against the side of the truck. She clutched his shoulders, trying to get good purchase as he began to forge into her.

Ty broke the kiss out of desperation for air. He was already feeling lightheaded. A common condition whenever he sank himself into Tessa's warm, wet heaven. Her inner muscles sucked him in, grasping tightly. Slowly he began to move, taking her with long, controlled thrusts. Back and forth, he flexed his hips with deliberate intention.

It was too much. Her body was already in shreds from Chase's fucking. Her body couldn't hold it in. Her muscles contracted hard as a wave of pleasure, so sharp it was painful, raced over her. Pure, untainted bliss crashed through her and she exploded at the seams. She slumped forward into his arms, her forehead crashing into his shoulders as she gasped for breath. Her chest wasn't the only thing heaving.

Ty continued to pound into her. His pace was quickening, his strength growing despite the added weight of her limp body. It didn't stop him, but he didn't last much longer, either. Within a minute she felt him stiffen, impaling her deep, as far as he could go. The hot jet of his release flooded her body as he groaned with his pleasure.

They stayed that way for several long moments, hearts racing, lungs heaving, arms wrapped tightly around each other. Finally, Ty groaned again and stepped back, lifting her off his cock and placing her back onto her feet.

"Are you all right?" His husky voice warmed her almost as much as the consideration he showed by keeping his arms locked around her, holding her until he was sure her legs would support her.

"Be better if I had my dress on." Tessa smiled, her own voice hoarse.

"Nothing stops the sass," Chase commented, drawing her eyes to where he was leaning against the truck. There was a glimmer in his smoky eyes that she knew well. Watching Ty fuck her always got him hot and from the lightning streaking through his gaze, Tessa knew she had to get him into the apartment fast or risk a repeat performance there on the side of the street.

Her dress was dangling over his arm and with her motivation in place, she found the strength to stand.

"My dress, sir." Tessa used her most haughty tone.

"Allow me." Chase stepped forward. While he dressed her, Ty buttoned himself back up.

"Now don't get too comfortable." Chase took Tessa's arm and began escorting her to the stairs. "You won't be wearing it for long."

Ty hadn't even shut the door before Chase was lifting Tessa up. She found herself draped over his hard shoulder as he carried her to the bedroom, barbarian-style. A second after he tossed her onto the bed, the phone rang.

"Ignore it."

Chase's order was unnecessary. She wasn't interested in talking to whoever was calling. Chase flopped onto the bed, bouncing into position next to her. Immediately he began to nibble on her neck, whispering lewd and exciting suggestions in her ear while his hands tried to make quick work of her clothes.

"Tessa!" Marcie's loud voice screeched out of her answering machine, piercing the mood. "Stop fornicating and get the hell over here! Linda is losing it and I'm not exactly sure what to do. I'm going to call again in five minutes!"

Chapter 13

Tessa stretched, enjoying the sensation of waking up. She'd always been a morning person, even more so this past week. There was nothing like waking up to seeing a man stretched out beside her.

She ignored the pang of her heart that there was only one man breathing deeply in her bed and not two. She wasn't going to let the upset of last night, when she had gotten home from Marcie's to find only Chase waiting for her, ruin her morning.

She'd been a little crabby, though not completely, because Ty was missing. She had been stiff and tired when she'd walked through the door and Chase storming into the kitchen, yelling at her, hadn't helped her disposition.

It didn't matter to her that she had accidentally left her cell on vibrate and missed his calls. She hadn't cared that it was three in the morning and he had been trying to reach her for hours. She'd matched him shout for shout until he said those five magic words, "I was worried about you."

Then her annoyance had dissolved and she had melted into his arms. It was his first verbal acknowledgement of what she had felt growing stronger all week. Suddenly all her aches disappeared and she was floating through Utopia once more.

At least, she had been until Chase had carried her into the bedroom and she realized Ty had left. It seemed silly and stupid to be upset by his absence, but that hadn't stopped her heart from seizing. The sharp pain in her chest made her realize how vulnerable she had become to them.

Tessa shook her head to clear it of those thoughts. She was going to be happy and enjoy having Chase with her. She studied him while he slept, her eyes catching on the erection tenting the bed sheets. Now that was something worth focusing on. Tessa debated for a moment whether to wake Chase first, but decided against it.

There had been several mornings this past week when she had awakened to find a hard cock sliding into her. Not strangely, that had coincided with her increase in erotic dreams. Perhaps it was time to give him his own erotic fantasy.

Tessa smiled, liking that idea.

* * * *

Chase sighed as Tessa's hot mouth worked its way down his body, following the soft, gentle caresses of her hands. Her wicked little tongue came out to tease his flat nipples. Her teeth scraped over the hardened nubs just enough to send streaks of heat through his body.

The tendrils ignited into full flames as her fingers feathered their way down to his cock as she teased him. When those warm, mischievous fingers curled around his balls, rolling them in their tender sack, it felt like a red-hot poker had seared him. He jerked, moaning with pleasure.

She giggled, her breath teasing the head of his cock, causing his hips to strain upward, blindly seeking her mouth. Her hand tightened on his balls, squeezing until he groaned and twisted beneath her touch. She giggled again, moving her hand up to wrap around his cock. She clasped his sensitive head, pulling it slightly as her hand slid down his length.

"You like that?" Her voice was soft, sultry, a tease to his senses. "Do you want my mouth? You want me to suck your cock? Lick it, nibble on it and swallow everything when you come?"

"Yes."

Chase panted, excited by her words. Slowly, she sank her mouth over his erection, her tongue tasting every inch as her lips captured him. Her lips tightened as her head rose, sucking with amazing strength.

"That's perfect, baby." Chase groaned. He tried reaching for her, but his arms wouldn't obey his command. Responding to his silent struggle, she nipped him lightly with her teeth. Chase jerked and cursed. A moment later, he groaned again as she swallowed as much of his dick as she could fit down her throat. Her hands came up to close over the rest of him.

Slowly at first, she began to suck him, her hands working in rhythm with her mouth and tongue. His cockhead hit the back of her throat as her motion sped up and she swallowed.

"Do that again," he pleaded.

She obeyed and Chase growled. The sensations washing through him were too much, too intense. It was heaven, filling

*her wet mouth with his cock, having her take him as deep and
fast as she could, but he wanted more.*

*"Your pussy," Chase gasped, fighting to hold back his
release. "Let me ...have...oh, God, baby!"*

* * * *

Chase tipped his head back and let out a roar as the mind-
shattering orgasm washed over him. The lava-hot eruption left
him feeling strong and powerful.

He collapsed back onto the bed, letting the afterglow of his
climax consume him. It was only when he heard Tessa's
laughter that he opened his eyes to the reality he had thought
was a dream.

Chase recognized the feel of the fuzzy cuffs around his
wrists. Tilting his head back, he grinned at the sight of his arms
chained to her bed. He looked back at Tessa. There was a
sparkle in her eyes and he knew she was waiting for his
reaction.

"If you think that's going to get you out of paying up what
you owe from last night, darlin', you're sadly mistaken."

"Hmm. What are you going to do about it, big boy?"

"Delaying only adds interest to the loan, baby."

Tessa laughed and the sound was pure joy to Chase,
warming him in ways he had never felt before. This was what he
wanted to wake to for the rest of his life. Well, maybe without
the cuffs, at least not on *his* wrists.

"I think I can afford the deferred payments. For right now,
you're my slave boy."

"And what would you have your slave do?" Chase drawled in that husky voice that sent shivers down Tessa's spine.

She knew what she wanted, but she had never been so forward as she was about to be. It was another first for her. Biting her lower lip, she straddled his chest. Her heart was racing as she angled her cunt over his face.

"Please me, slave," she ordered in her most commanding tone.

With the first lap of his tongue, pleasure shot through her. She jerked from the force of the sensation, lifting her hips away from him. Beneath her, Chase chuckled.

"I can't give you what you want, sweetheart, unless you stay put."

Tessa settled back down on his face, holding the headboard to keep her in position. It was hard, really hard, to stay still as he began to lick and tease her pussy. His clever tongue swirled over her hot opening before pressing open her folds to find the sensitive nub hidden at the top.

Chase attacked her clit, sucking it between his teeth and tormenting it with his tongue. In seconds, her hips jerked again, pulling away from Chase.

"Damn it, woman!" Chase growled. "Come back here!"

Tessa dropped back down to his waiting mouth. Chase showed her no mercy. Beginning again as he had left off, it wasn't a whole minute before Tessa was gasping, lifting back off his mouth.

"I think you need to be the one tied down, baby, because you are having all sorts of problems."

Tessa couldn't deny it. As much as she wanted to return to the tongue-fucking he was giving her, she knew she couldn't take any more. Her body was too undisciplined to ride his mouth all the way to the end, but there was something else she could ride to completion.

Chase laughed as he watched her lever herself over his cock. He knew just what his revenge would be when he got free of the cuffs. There would be no escape for her then.

The feel of her hot, tight sheath sucking him deep inside cut off his thoughts. Chase closed his eyes as the flames of renewed desire licked up his body. He wanted to feel her riding him hard and fast, but she moved over him with long, slow strokes that drove him mad. Growling his displeasure, he thrust his hips upward, trying to slam himself into her.

Tessa laughed above him, obviously enjoying his aggression. When he repeated the motion, he was pleased to hear her laughter turn into a groan. Her body responded to his demand, her pussy tightening around his cock, the muscles beginning the contractions that would suck him into the abyss.

Her motions picked up speed and she rode him with a quickness that matched the flames burning through his body. His balls were on fire, teetering on the edge of an explosion he was sure would rip his woman in two. Chase fought the urge, trying to hold back until she found her own release.

Then she was screaming as the tight fist of her sheath convulsed around him. The pressure was too much. His hips jerked once, twice, shafting himself right to the back of her little cunt as his hot seed erupted from his body. His entire body pulled tight for a moment before his muscles spasmed uncontrollably under his release.

Tessa collapsed on top of him, her body wet with sweat, her muscles shaking in harmony with his. This was it, what he had been looking for his whole life, absolute nirvana. Nothing had ever come close to this feeling. It was the same every time they came together.

Chase wished now more than before that his arms were free. He liked to hold her. That was right. He, Chase Dunn, wanted to cuddle. The shrill sound of her phone ringing broke the magic spell. Tessa groaned and shifted.

"Ah, shit." She lifted her head.

"Ignore it. It'll stop soon."

"I can't." Tessa lifted away from him. "It might be Linda."

Chapter 14

It hadn't been Linda on the phone. It had been Mr. Jack Humphries, Tessa's lawyer. She had been less than thrilled to have the morning pleasantries interrupted by the attorney.

Humphries explained that Banning & Dunn had sent him a compromise. Tessa had summarily dismissed the idea. Humphries had insisted she come to his office and take a look.

Tessa had freed Chase and reluctantly gotten herself ready to go to war. Chase's curiosity in her destination had ended when she had explained it was her lawyer's office. Her ongoing battle with Banning & Dunn was the only topic both Ty and Chase refused to discuss.

Actually, that wasn't the only thing they hadn't discussed. None of them had brought up the idea of a relationship. Not that she took that as a hesitation on their part. The conversation had simply never evolved.

Tessa certainly wasn't going to start it. She hated relationship talks. They never went smoothly. It was safer to leave well enough alone. After all, things were going so good. She didn't want to be disillusioned of her belief that they cared.

What else was she to think when they kept showing up at her door every night? She knew they worked in construction, but they had been padding their wallets with extra cash as paid escorts, or had been until they had met her. Tessa didn't doubt Ty and Chase could be out there making a lot of money with other women or men if they wanted. Instead, they were choosing to spend their evenings with her, not making a dime. That had to mean something.

Then where had Ty gone last night?

Tessa cringed at the thought. Despite the fog of happiness she had immersed herself in, Tessa was rational enough to admit that there was something going on with Ty. He was just as passionate as Chase, enjoyed her company just as much, and certainly liked to cuddle.

Still, there was something wrong that she couldn't completely identify. She wanted to say it was a level of intensity, but Ty was just naturally more reserved and brooding than Chase. She would catch him looking at her sometimes. His blue eyes dark and guarded.

Thoughts of Ty and Chase consumed her as she drove to her lawyer's office. Humphries was very excited about Banning & Dunn's offer and dragged her right into his office. She only listened half-heartedly as he explained the developer's latest proposal with unusual enthusiasm.

"Well, what do you think?" Mr. Humphries drew her attention back to him.

The short balding man had an expectant look on his rounded face. Despite his age, he had boyish features that Tessa was sure helped endear him to juries. He looked eternally optimistic and just had that air that made people relax.

"Do you like the drawings?"

Tessa's eyes dropped back to the papers littering Humphries' desk. She surveyed the well-done images depicting the changes Banning & Dunn had made to their development plans. The style was completely different from the original set.

It was a very upscale design, but gone was the homage to glass and metal. While the new drawings still showed off a lot of windows, the modern style had been replaced with a more sophisticated approach to classic lines.

As a nod to the historical architecture, the old brick buildings that lined South Bend had been incorporated into the design. They would make the foundation of the condominium complex. The alleys between the buildings would be enclosed and the complex would encompass the whole block.

The interior showed how the developer planned to turn the old buildings into shops that would service the new condominium complex. The rear facades of the buildings would be opened up and renovated, but the style would remain basically the same, as would the front of the buildings facing the streets.

Her own office and apartment would remain untouched, except her private entrance in back would be eliminated. There was even a guarantee that her rent would not change for as long as she continued to lease the space. It all looked and sounded too good to be true.

"What do you think?" Tessa glanced back at Humphries.

"I think it's amazing." He gave a nervous little laugh.

"So this is real?"

"Oh, it's real all right, Miss Miller." He assured her. "All the paperwork is in order. If you approve of their plans and agree to drop your lawsuit, they'll drop theirs and begin development."

Tessa frowned and looked down at the drawings again. She knew she should be happy, excited even. This was what she'd wanted. She had accomplished her main goal, saving the old buildings. The problem was she didn't trust Banning & Dunn.

They had the classic corporate attitude to developing areas, gut and rebuild tacky, cheap buildings that they could sell at a premium. Tessa knew there were a lot of headaches coming for anybody who tried to renovate an old house. It was stressful, time consuming and, normally, expensive. She doubted Banning & Dunn had that kind of stamina, much less desire to see the project through as planned. This could well be the Trojan horse, but instead of sneaking in, they were sneaking her out.

"You will have to vacate the premises while the building is under construction, but Banning & Dunn is willing to subsidize your temporary location," Humphries explained. "You'll pay them your normal rent and they'll cover the rest."

"That seems a little excessive."

"You don't argue with excess when you're on the receiving end."

"But I do get to question why." Tessa frowned. "Why are they conceding defeat? You told me our case wasn't likely to win. They had the position of power, so why bow down to us?"

"Money," Humphries answered succinctly. "They may win the court case in the end, but I could make that a very long exercise. Time is money for developers, not to mention the legal fees they would have to pay for going to court. Why bother with all that, when they could reach a cheap and timely compromise."

"I see."

"So? Are we compromising?" Humphries asked expectantly.

"And we're guaranteed they're not going to change the plans later?"

"Nothing is absolute in this case, but we're as close as we can get."

"Okay." Tessa sighed. "I'll compromise."

"Great." Humphries clapped his hands. "I've got all the paperwork right here."

"You can leave out the part about the rent and temporary housing."

"What?" Humphries, who had been collecting the drawings littering his desk, paused. "Why? I think you should accept. Construction could take a while and when they're done, the rent in this complex is going to be very high."

"I wouldn't be returning to South Bend once the project is complete," Tessa assured him. "I don't have any desire to live or work in a large complex."

"You'll forgive me, Miss Miller, but I thought you wanted to save your location."

"I wanted to save the buildings. These plans accomplish that, for the most part. You have given me the impression that this is the best outcome I can achieve. I'll sign whatever you need me to and be happy with that."

Mr. Humphries stared at her for a long moment, his blue eyes wide with surprise. He threw it off and quickly started to go through the paperwork. Tessa could sense his relief that this matter was settled as he had her sign form after form.

Humphries had made it quite clear during their first meeting that he considered her case weak, if not impossible, to win. He had suggested she save her money. That had been the reason she had hired him. Tessa appreciated his honesty, even if she was ignoring his advice.

Tessa wasn't rich, but she spent her money on what was important to her. Saving those historic buildings had been a high priority and she had accomplished that goal.

A half hour later, with all the papers signed, Tessa wrote Humphries a check for services rendered. She silently thanked God for her new client. With his check, her account was not on empty, as it would have been.

As he escorted her out into his small waiting room, the lawyer assured her he would get everything back to Banning & Dunn by the end of the day. They said their good-byes and Tessa turned to leave. She was passing the small coffee table littered with old newspapers when a picture caught her eye. She felt all the blood draining out of her head as her eyes focused on the image.

It can't be.

With trembling hands, she picked up the dated society section. There was no denying it. It was Ty in the photograph on the society page with a gorgeous blonde on his arm. Her breath caught and she couldn't take her eyes off the woman. She was perfect, not a single strand of hair out of place. The long, elegant dress showed off her toned body, making her appear long and lean. The only fat on the woman was in her well-developed chest.

She's just a client. Tessa assured herself of that as her eyes began scanning the article for Ty's name. When she found it, she felt as if she had been hit in the stomach.

Olivia Duncan and her longtime escort, Tyler Banning...

Tyler Banning. Tyler Banning, as in Banning & Dunn? Banning & Dunn Construction?

Chase and Ty?

Chapter 15

"So."

"So," Ty echoed as the elevator doors closed.

"You sent the plans to Tessa's lawyer?" Chase had been meaning to talk to Ty all day, but between one thing and another, he hadn't gotten a chance.

"Yep."

"I didn't think they were ready."

"I thought it was a priority."

"And?" Chase prodded after Ty fell silent.

"And she accepted the new design."

Chase heaved a sigh of relief. "So that's done."

He hated lying to Tessa, would do anything to see her happy, anything but let her go. That meant he had to devise a plan for telling her the truth that preserved his place in her bed. He was hopeful the new designs for the condominium project would mitigate his deception.

Chase didn't fool himself into thinking there wasn't going to be hell to pay, but Tessa loved him and Ty. It was there in her eyes, her smile, in the way she responded to their touch. He loved Tessa and was certain that would assure a happy ending to whatever tantrum was coming his way.

Ty was a different matter.

"What're you doing tonight?" Chase eyed Ty's expensive suit, instinctively knowing he was not going to Tessa's.

"Got plans with Olivia."

"Why don't you dump that snooty bitch? Come with me to Tessa's."

"Don't go there." Ty cast a dirty look at Chase. "And don't call Olivia a bitch."

"Why the hell not?"

"Because she's my girlfriend," Ty snapped.

"That's not what I meant and you know it."

"We deceived her, Chase. How do you think she's going to react when she finds out?"

Chase shrugged. "She's going to have a fit, but she'll get over it."

"She'll get over it?" Ty barked out a harsh laugh.

"Yeah, she will, and you know why?"

"I'm afraid to ask."

"Because she loves us. And you know what else?" Chase didn't wait for Ty to answer. "I love her. You do, too, but you don't want to admit it."

"Do you hear yourself? You're talking as if we have a real relationship."

"Yep."

"With both of us."

"Yep."

"That's ridiculous." Ty stared at Chase in disbelief. "Let's just say we tell Tessa who we really are and she forgives us for deceiving her, what you are thinking is…impossible."

"Why? We've shared women before?"

"For the night! Some for a few weeks, but that's just a fling. Not for a lifetime."

"I don't see what the problem is. We've lived together before, we've shared women, now we'd be living together and sharing a woman."

"What about marriage? Kids? Those sorts of things?"

"Well, I'd let you marry her, because I know how excited your mom would be, and I think we'd make perfect fathers. Between us, the kids would have the best of everything." Chase paused and shrugged again. "Of course, hopefully they would look like me."

"You're living in a dream world."

Ty looked up as the elevator doors slid open. Olivia was waiting by the front desk. She was dressed in a designer suit. She looked stylish, not a hair out of place, not a single wrinkle in her clothes. Perfect.

"You do what you want," Chase said as Ty stepped out of the elevator. "But I'm not letting Tessa go."

Before Ty could respond to that, the elevator doors slid shut. He glared at his warped reflection in the metal as the cab whooshed Chase lower to the parking level. Ty knew where Chase was headed and damnit, he wanted to beside him.

With a sense of resignation, Ty turned to look at Olivia. She smiled in welcome. It was a controlled expression, portraying happiness, but no real excitement. Tessa's smile was always full of joy, a double-dimpled delight. If it were Tessa who was greeting him after a week of separation, Ty suspected she would be squealing and running to throw herself into his arms.

Not Tyler Banning's arms, Ty's arms. That little distinction was the cause of all his problems, all his guilt. He'd set things as right as possible with Tessa without hurting her unnecessarily. Now it was time to do the same with Olivia.

"Tyler—"

"Tyler Banning?" A uniformed police officer came strutting into the lobby, followed by his partner.

"Yes?" Ty frowned at the large, uniformed man.

"I'm sorry sir. You're going to have to come down to the station and answer a few questions."

"What for?" Olivia demanded before Ty could ask.

The officer directed his answer at Ty. "You've been accused of prostitution." He stepped back and gestured between him and his partner. "If you don't mind, sir."

* * * *

By the time Ty finished collecting his personal effects from the desk officer, Chase had his laughter under control. Mostly under control. The chuckles seeped out, gaining in force as Ty slammed the passenger door of Chase's truck.

Ty didn't know what was worse, dealing with the hurt in Olivia's eyes, the accusations she'd flung at him before storming out of the station or the pure merriment in Chase's tone as he laughed and joked with the cops.

"I'm glad somebody is having a good night," Ty sneered as Chase slid behind the wheel.

"This is priceless."

"No, actually, it cost me five hundred and sixty dollars to get out of that cell and it's going to cost me even more to keep it out of the courtroom," Ty snapped. "God, if Tessa was here now I'd blister her ass so bad she wouldn't be able to sit for a whole year!"

"Actually, it's your ass that might be in trouble if you end up in jail."

"You're looking for a fight, aren't you?"

"Ah, come on, man. You know that if it had been me arrested for prostitution, you'd be laughing your ass off."

"At least you would have deserved it," Ty muttered.

"I'm not the one who took the four hundred and fifty dollars." Chase started the engine.

"I meant to return it!"

"But you didn't." Chase snickered. "And our little Tessa used that fact to her advantage."

"She's not ours!"

"Okay, mine. Better?"

No, it wasn't better. Ty didn't know what he was feeling. Anger, yeah, but it wasn't the rage that he should have felt at having been arrested. Part of him felt relieved, strangely enough. Now he didn't have to wonder or worry over Tessa's reaction to finding out the truth.

"Yes, siree, my little Tessa has quite a wicked sense of retribution." Chase laughed.

"She's not yours!"

"She's not ours, not mine, what is she then? Yours?"

"She's not either of ours."

"Doesn't work that way." Chase shook his head. "I told you before, I'm in love with her and I'm not letting her go."

"It's infatuation, that's all. It will pass. I'm not going to ruin my life just for lust, even if it is the strongest I've ever felt."

"Ruin your life." Chase snorted. "You don't need Tessa to do that, you're doing a good job of that on your own."

"What the hell does that mean?"

"It means that you have all these plans and, for the most part, they're good plans, but you forgot the most important thing when you set the goals."

"Really? What was that?"

"Happiness, my friend."

"Happiness." Ty shook his head and turned to look out the window. He was happy, wasn't he? "It doesn't matter. She hates our guts."

"No. She doesn't hate us."

"Oh, I see. Having me arrested was a sign of affection, is that it?"

"No. It was a challenge." Chase looked over at him and grinned. "Ball's in our court now."

"In our court? You think this is a damn game."

"No. I think we honestly hurt Tessa and that kills me inside, but I'm not going to slink off and lick my wounds. I'm going to make her see that no matter what, she belongs with me. She belongs with you, too, but that's your decision to make. I will tell you this, Ty: You make it and you keep it. I'm not going to let your insecurities hurt her. We've already hurt her enough."

"I never meant to hurt her," Ty said quietly, feeling the anger and aggression draining out of him. "I don't want to hurt her anymore. That's why I think we should stay away. Let her get over us and go on."

"It doesn't work that way, Ty."

"You know that for a fact?"

"I saw her face last night when she realized you had left."

Ty flinched at that. He'd had to leave last night, he'd needed to think. They had lied to her, deceived her in the worst possible way. For the past week, he had lived in alternating worlds of heaven and hell.

Heaven was being with Tessa, hearing her laugh, listening to her unconventional viewpoints, holding her close while she slept. It had also been hell, every moment knowing that one day her eyes would darken with betrayal and accusation and love would turn to hate.

That moment was today and he had never felt so empty inside as he did now. He wanted to believe Chase, believe they could overcome this, that they could figure out a way to make it all work out so they could spend the rest of their lives suspended in the joy of the past week.

Ty was nothing if not practical. There was no way this could work out. It just wasn't possible. Even if they could get beyond this moment, happiness, like love, never lasted.

"So?" Chase braked for a red light and turned to look at him. "Are you in or out?"

Chapter 16

12:48

Tessa sighed as she looked from the clock to the phone. It sat silently, mocking her for whatever wayward hope she was holding that it would ring. She'd spent the night alternating between telling herself she never wanted to hear from those two bastards again and wishing they would call so she could tell them never to call her.

After leaving Humphries' office, she had come home to do a little research on the Web. Her suspicions had been confirmed, but that was not the worst of it. Olivia Duncan was not just Ty's girlfriend. She was damn-near his fiancée.

They were the darling couple of the town. They'd been together for over a year and expectations were high that an engagement was soon to be announced.

A whole fucking year!

Tessa clenched her jaw as shudders of rage passed through her. It was that idea, the knowledge that he was seriously involved with another woman, that had sent her over the edge.

It hadn't been hard to get her old high school friends, Jace and Alex, to help her yank Ty's chain in their official roles as police officers. It had only required a little bribery. She'd agreed to help set Jace up with Marcie and he had been only too willing to haul in Ty for suspicion of prostitution.

Another good friend, Janice had been more than willing to be waiting to cover the story for the early morning issue of the *Times*. No bribery needed.

Janice had called two hours ago to tell her that Ty had pretty much confessed. Of course, in his version of things it was just a misunderstanding, but he didn't deny that he had allowed her to think he was a paid escort. He had been formally arrested when he'd agreed she had given him four hundred fifty dollars in cash for sexual services rendered.

Under arrest. The minute Janice had said those words, Tessa had been struck dumb. Never had she thought it would come to that.

Suddenly, her impulsive action appeared less than intelligent. Ty was no doubt furious. Wait until he saw the paper tomorrow. Maybe she should be packing a bag and finding some false identification to flee the country with.

One thing was for sure, there would be no going back now. They were truly, officially over.

Good! Good riddance! Tessa thought it, wanted to believe it, but the ache in her heart was unrelenting. It told her how much she cared and she called herself stupid, gullible and every other insult she could think of.

However mad Ty was, she doubted he was hurting. He had Olivia to fill any void. Chase had whoever was the new flavor of the week.

Tessa had learned all about Chase's playboy ways. Not that she was shocked. She had certainly known he was a helpless flirt and benefited from his experience at pleasing women.

Still, it was one thing to know it and another to see him in picture after picture with model-perfect women. It figured. She should have known something was wrong. She was definitely not the type two super-hunky men just fell in love with.

Her only defense was that she'd been too busy enjoying herself to think rationally. Oh, how that was biting her on the ass now. They had played her for a fool and she'd happily gone along.

Tessa growled. She wished they were here just so she could throw them the hell out of her apartment, out of her life. Tessa looked up at the still-silent phone.

Yeah, that was exactly what I would do if they were here.

Ah, hell. Tessa dropped her head into her hands. She didn't know what she would do. The surging emotional tides raking through her conflicted then coalesced, constantly changing every few minutes. The upheaval left her drained and exhausted.

They weren't going to call, Tessa just had to accept that and go to bed. She looked up, through the darken doorway to her bedroom where the queen bed was made up with crisp, clean linens.

She didn't want to sleep there. That would be depressing. There was no peace to be had in that bed. The minute her head hit the pillow her mind would spin out of control. It would insist on replaying the past week, picking everything apart and fueling her turbulent emotions. As much as she would desire to escape into the oblivion of sleep, her brain would not stop.

No. Tonight she needed some help.

* * * *

A stray stand of hair was tickling her cheek, annoying her. Tessa tried to brush it away, but her arm refused to cooperate. She grumbled slightly over the complication and settled for jerking her head, trying to throw off the strand.

That worked. Sighing, she settled back into the mattress. Time slowed and elongated as she came to the blurred edge of sleep. The strand of hair returned. Tessa tilted her head further away from it, mumbling obscenities when it refused to leave her alone.

The sound of male laughter filtered through her groggy brain. She recognized that sound. Cursing, she demanded Chase leave her alone. That only earned her another spate of laughter.

Whatever he was tickling her with moved lower, down her neck and toward her chest. Tessa tried to swat the annoyance away, but still her arms refused to move. They were stuck and she knew just who to blame.

"Damn it, Chase!"

Tessa tried to sit up, but her body didn't move. The only thing that lifted were her eyelids. It wasn't Chase, but Ty who was standing beside the bed. That didn't matter to her.

"Leave me alone!" Tessa spat, her eyes falling closed. "I'm tired."

The last was mumbled through a yawn. Thankfully, he obeyed, allowing her to drift back to the sweet blackness of sleep.

Ty watched her features relax, her breathing even out. This was not the response he had been expecting. Normally she woke up aware, even in the middle of the night. He'd anticipated a real fight once her eyes opened and she saw just who was in her bedroom. That was why they had tied her down, to make sure she stayed put.

His eyes shifted to the nightstand where the box of over-the-counter sleeping pills sat next to a nearly empty glass of water. He looked down at the rose in his hand. He was going to need something a lot more bracing to shock her out of the fog of the pills.

* * * *

Tessa was tugged back from the peaceful emptiness of sleep by the gentle feel of hands running up the sides of her legs. This interruption was greeted with a lack of rancor the previous one had received. The slow, sensual glide of the work-roughened hands both excited and soothed her lethargic body.

Tessa sighed, stretching slightly as his touch slid over her thighs. They drifted up over her sides as the heavy weight of a male body settled down on top of her. His chest hair tickled her hardened nipples. His thick erection snuggled into her pussy. She breathed out harshly as her body began to awake to the pleasures of the flesh.

Her skin shivered with pleasure, hypersensitive to the feel of her lover above, delighting in the way his hard angles settled into her soft curves. Her mind was still hazy, not aware enough to analyze the moment, just awake enough to enjoy it.

Warm, soft lips settled in the indentation between her neck and shoulder, nibbling, licking, his teeth raking over her tender skin. In a soft, husky voice, Ty began to describe in vivid detail what he wanted to do to her. Her stomach tightened, her pussy creamed at his erotic suggestions.

Subtly he began to move, rubbing himself into her. His erection rocked inward, pressing against her pussy lips, dividing them, exposing her clit to the slow grind of his cock. The teasing motion drew a ragged cry from her lips as her hips arched, pushing her sensitive nub more firmly against his hardness.

Her body tightened as his hips flexed with greater strength, increased speed. It was erotic, an exotic pleasure she had never thought could be so intense. A harsh cry was wrung from her lips as she strained to match his rhythm.

She was hot and wet, and his balls were near bursting. Ty's engorged cock throbbed, demanding that he cease this torment and plunge deep into his woman, pump them both into orgasm. He couldn't do that, not yet, not without her consent.

With long, heated motions he continued to stroke himself against her swollen clit. The proof of her escalating desire coated his length in warm, sticky cream. She was tense beneath him.

Her eyes popped open. Wide, glazed eyes darkened with desire stared unseeing at him. A strangled scream barely escaped her mouth as he felt her shudder and convulse with her climax.

She floated in the mind-numbing sea of ecstasy, never wanting to sink back to reality. The aftershocks of the mind-shattering detonation that had ripped her world apart continued to ripple through her. The deep striations of pleasure scored her body and left her vibrating with a need for more, much more.

It didn't last. Sink she did as bits and pieces congealed, forcing her to remember. Reality slammed into her hard. The erotic pleasure of the moment was snuffed out as her bliss soured in the heat of righteous indignation that boiled to life in her blood.

Chapter 17

Ty heard the warning growl and knew that the pleasantries were over, at least for now. He forced himself to remain calm and relaxed, focused on the plan. It wasn't the plan Ty would have devised, but he had deferred to Chase.

"What the hell do you think you are doing?" she demanded, right on cue.

"What does it feel like?" He nuzzled her neck, delighted when she shivered in response. She may be mad as hell, but she couldn't deny her body's reaction to his touch.

"Get the hell off me!" She bucked and twisted beneath him like a wild thing, fighting her bonds. His lips paused over her madly beating pulse, his tongue coming out to taste her skin there. She jerked and cursed at him.

"Mmmm." Ty ground his pelvis into hers, making her gasp and twist. "You taste so sweet."

"Stop that!"

"Ah, sweetheart." Ty lifted his head to see that her eyes were now flashing with green lightning. Her full lips were pressed into the thin lines of anger. It was her stubborn little chin, raised in defiance, that worried him the most.

"Get off me and get the hell out of my apartment!" Tessa hissed. "I don't want anything to do with you ever again!"

"Nothing?" He brushed her clit with his cock. Her response was instant. She arched her hips, but not away from him. "Are you sure about that?"

"Yes," she snarled, despite her body's response. "I'm positive."

"I know you have good reason to hate us, Tessa."

"Gee, why would I hate you? I just love to be lied to, deceived, manipulated and humiliated."

"Technically, we never lied."

"Excuse me?" Tessa gaped, completely taken aback.

"God, baby, you're so soft." Ty leaned down to rub his cheek against hers.

"Don't try to distract me!" Tessa fought not to give in to the lure of his touch.

"If you will recall the first time we met, I tried more than once to tell you the truth. You kept interrupting me," Ty whispered against her ear, nibbling on the lobe.

"Ah!" Tessa shrieked. She fought her bounds, enraged not only by his words, but also by the effect he had on her senses. "You did not just blame this all on me!"

"I'm just saying." Ty shrugged, knowing that would piss her off even more. It was part of Chase's plan. He was going to get her as mad as possible, riled into a full-fledged tantrum, let her get it out of her system.

"Oh, you better hope these binds hold, Tyler Banning. So help me God, if I get my hands on you—"

"I love it when you touch me." Ty began kissing his way down her neck. "Your touch drives me insane, makes me hotter than I've ever been. It's all I—"

"Shut up!" She meant to yell it, but the words came out as a high-pitched squeak.

Despite her mind's commands to ignore what he was doing, her body was eagerly anticipating the moment when those warm, talented lips would close over her nipple. He was close, so close.

"Come on, sweetheart." He lifted his head. "You have to admit that from the moment you opened the door, you didn't give us a single chance to get a word in. Hell, I had to kiss you just to shut you up."

"And what about the sex? Was that just to shut me up too?" Tessa panted, not about to be ruled by her body's lust for him.

"Ah, no. That was just for the fun of it. And you have to admit it was pretty fun."

His hands came up to massage her breasts, his thumbs rolling her nipples in slow circles. The small touch echoed through her body, sending another round of shivers racing over her as her back arched into his touch, seeking more.

"Leave me alone," Tessa ground through clenched teeth, fighting the desire that was changing the heat in her blood from anger to arousal.

"No can do, baby."

"Why the hell not?" Tessa panted, struggling to stay focused on their argument. It wasn't easy. He was rotating his hips, rubbing her clit with his erection.

"Because, you love me, baby."

"No. No. No." Tessa shook her head.

"Yes, you do. You've fallen hopelessly, helplessly in love with Chase and me."

"No. I hate you."

"What do you think, Chase? She telling the truth?"

Tessa's eyes popped open, her head jerking in the direction Ty looked. He had so thoroughly captured her attention, she'd completely forgotten to check for the other one. There he sat, looking ruggedly handsome in the armchair beside her closet door.

He was naked. His hardened cock rose like a trophy from his lap as he waited his turn. The warm glint in his eyes told her how much he was enjoying the show.

"I think she's lying," Chase drawled.

"I am not," Tessa groaned out, losing the fight to keep her hips still. They flexed and rotated, matching Ty's rhythm. Even as her body crumbled beneath his seductive movements, she still managed to argue. "I could never love a man who lied to me."

"We didn't come here intending to lie to you." Chase shrugged. "Everything changed when you opened that door. You were so beautiful and engaging."

"I was mesmerized by your smile," Ty leaned down to whisper, dropping little butterfly kisses across her lips, working his way up her cheek to her eyelids and brow. "Enchanted by the joy in your eyes. I know I should have told you the truth then. My only excuse is that you bewitched me as no other woman ever has."

"You don't really expect me to believe that crap, do you?" Tessa's words lacked the bite she wanted them to have, thanks to the breathy desire in her voice.

"It's the truth." He cupped her face, tilting her head back to force her to look at him.

"Really? You were so stunned by my beauty that you couldn't get around to telling me the truth? Not just that night, but for an entire week?"

Ty could see it in her eyes. The anger was still there, but the hurt was taking over. He could hear it in her tone, too.

"If we had told you the truth the next day, you would have thrown us out. Then we never would have had the chance to discover what was between us."

"Your other girlfriend might be stupid enough to buy into a handful of sweet words, but I know who you really are. I'm not that dumb."

Other girlfriend? She had to be referring to Olivia, and how Tessa knew about her, he didn't know. The accusation hit hard and he cringed. Her eyes narrowed on the motion, flaring with renewed heat. Things had just slipped out of his control.

"What? Didn't think I knew about your high-society blonde?"

"We broke up."

"Really? When?" Tessa demanded, blinking rapidly to hold back the tears that were beginning to burn her eyes.

"Well..." Ty faltered.

"Oh, so it's not really over, right?"

"No, it is," Ty responded quickly. "It's just..."

"Jesus, Ty." Chase sighed in the background. "You're really fucking this one up. Look, Tessa, Olivia didn't mean anything to Ty."

"Didn't mean anything," Tessa repeated softly. "That's why he dated her for over a year, why half the city expected them to announce their engagement in the near future."

"Just a rumor," Chase dismissed with a wave of his hand. "Ty would never have married her."

"Yeah, right." Again the answer failed to reassure her, failed to soothe the now piercing pain in her heart.

"I wouldn't." Ty forced his way back into the conversation. "She didn't make me happy. Not like you do, Tessa."

"And you make me happy," Chase cut in. His voice sounded closer. The bed dipping to the right told her he had finally joined them. "We shouldn't have lied to you."

"We were afraid." Ty brought the conversation back to the direction they wanted. "Afraid of losing you."

"No," Tessa croaked, fighting them, fighting herself.

"I've never been so afraid of anything," Chase admitted.

She closed her eyes, unwilling to see Ty's expression on Chase's face. There were only so many lies her heart could take. "Don't say it."

Ty defied her. "We've fallen in love with you, Tessa."

"No." She denied him, had to. Those were the sucker words. They pulled at her heart, threatening to both heal and destroy.

"I love you, Tessa," Ty whispered.

They'd already hurt her more than anybody ever had. She couldn't risk it. Not again.

"I love you, Tessa," Chase echoed, kissing her gently on the cheek as the tears she could no longer control began to slip beneath her lids.

"Don't say that," she pleaded.

"You're so beautiful." Ty began tenderly lapping up her tears.

"So funny." Chase's tongue cleaned her other cheek.

"Intelligent."

"Sweet."

"Desirable."

"Perfect."

"And you're in love with us," Ty finished.

"No," Tessa shook her head, desperately fighting against what they were saying. She was supposed to be mad at them. They had hurt her. She would be a fool to make herself vulnerable to them again.

"Admit it, Tessa," Chase pushed.

"No."

"Tell us you love us."

"I wouldn't."

Ty looked at Chase, who gave him a quick grin. Things were going just the way they had planned. They had broken through her anger, gotten to the underlying hurt. Now all they had to do was replace the pain with pleasure.

Tessa sucked in a deep, ragged breath as she fought to control her emotions. They threatened to overwhelm her, destroy her. She couldn't let that happen. She had to stay firm in her denial.

First, she had to get her heart to stop beating so fast. It helped when Ty unexpectedly lifted off her. The cool air shocked her body back to reality, allowing her mind to clear and her breathing to even.

She could hear rustling and imagined that they were getting dressed. She kept her eyes closed, not trusting herself to confront the image of them leaving. The coming days would be hard, but she if she could get through the next few minutes then she would survive the next few weeks.

Chapter 18

Several tense moments passed, but instead of feeling her wrists and ankles being freed, Tessa felt a soft weight settle over her eyes. Instantly her eyes flew open, but all she could see was blackness.

"W-- what...?"

Tessa swallowed, trying to clear her throat of the anxiety constricting it. The potent aphrodisiac of excited apprehension made her pussy pulse and weep with renewed life. She wanted to tell Ty and Chase to go to hell, but the words got lost when a hand slid up her thigh.

She was not sure who was touching her. The loss of her sight made her feel vulnerable and added to her desire as those exploring hands dipped between her thighs, not even an inch from where she needed to be touched. Twin thumbs slid between her legs, opening her pussy and exposing her clit.

Those mischievous fingers pushed her nether lips inward, capturing her sensitive nub. The thumbs slid back and forth, using her own flesh to torment her clit. The slow, sensual teasing drove her insane.

Lips joined the fingers teasing her pussy, latching onto the little head peeking out and sucking lightly on it. She groaned as streaks of heat flamed up her body. Her hips instinctively arched into the touch.

A sudden, sharp slap against her clit made her jolt as much as her bindings would allow. The pain quickly flared into pleasure that soared to her nipples. When another slap landed against her ultra-sensitive nub, she flinched and yelped with a mixture of pain and pleasure.

With the third hit, she screamed. Just one more slap and her body would sing.

"You had me arrested."

That statement, given in a hard voice, was immediately followed by warm lips closing around her nipple, sucking it into a hard peak. Ty held her puckered tip with his teeth, rolling it with his tongue. She moaned and ground her head back into the mattress.

A second later an exquisite pain shot through her nipple. She screamed, thrashing about as she tried to dislodge whatever was pinching her distended peak. Quickly the pain transformed into a sizzling pleasure, leaving her panting under the force of the extreme sensations. Pleasure chased pain down her nerve endings, making every cell in her body fire and leaving her body a quivering mass on the verge of an unexpected climax.

He gave her a moment, just enough time to back off the edge of the precipice, before turning his attention to her other nipple. As his mouth closed over her other tender bud, Tessa remained tense, expecting pain to follow soon. Try as she might not to be lulled into a false sense of pleasure, her body melted under his talented lips as he spent more than a minute loving on her breast. Her back had just started to arch, a moan slipping past her guard when a second sharp pain shot from her other breast to her pussy.

"Now that's a sight." Chase's tone was ragged. The husky sound was a stroke to Tessa's already inflamed senses.

"Yeah," Ty agreed. "Maybe we should get her nipples pierced."

"And her clit. Then we can get her one of those chains that connect all three points."

Tessa swallowed hard, not wanting to like the image of what they were suggesting, but unable to stop the thrill the idea sent through her. She felt the bed depress to her right before Chase murmured in her ear.

"Imagine that, Tessa. We could pull you around by your chains and you would come at our command."

As if his point needed to be emphasized, he tugged on one of the nipple clamps, sending a riot of sensation through her body. Her muscles contracted, tightening with the expectation of climax.

Again, he stopped short and she was left gasping for breath as she fought the desire twisting her body into knots. It was a futile battle. The need refused to abate.

Chase's lusty chuckle sent a ripple of heat scorching down her belly. Knowing that they were watching her, imagining the image she must have made, only added to her excitement.

"Let's get her naked."

Chase's words confused her until she felt a warm, wet towel heat her pussy. Suddenly she understood perfectly what they intended to do.

A hand pressed the washrag into her pussy, rubbing the warmth into her. Its rough texture antagonized her clit, but did not give her enough friction. She held her breath when she felt the towel being lifted and shaving cream being applied.

For the next several minutes, she remained tense as the smooth feel of the razorblade slid over her most sensitive part. Afraid of being cut, she was grateful when the wet towel returned and she knew it was over.

"Mmm," Ty murmured as he removed the washrag. "What a pretty pink pussy you have. All swollen and wet, it tempts me to take a taste."

That was all the warning she got. With unleashed savagery, he attacked her cunt, his tongue flicking up her pussy, dividing her folds, circling her clit before sliding back down to bury itself deep inside her clenching sheath.

Again and again he tormented her. Not spending enough time on either her clit or her entrance to ease her burgeoning need, but enough to push her higher and higher, until she thought she would expire from the extreme sensations winding through her.

Tessa squirmed, panting for breath around the moans that escaped. She was so close to caving, to begging. Then, when she thought it couldn't get any more intense, he scraped her clit with his teeth. The small pain barely registered before Chase suddenly released the nipple clamps.

"Oh, God!"

Tessa screamed and thrashed as delicious, burning, painful pleasure consumed her. The violent climax rolled through her with a ferocity that threatened to kill her. It lasted longer than any she had ever experienced.

Finally, the tight grip of ecstasy lessened into a bone deep bliss. With a sigh, she collapsed back onto the bed. Her muscles were loose, her head pleasantly fogged, her eyelids too heavy to lift. The only part of her body putting forth any exertion was her chest. Her lungs heaved with deep breaths in an attempt to keep up with her pounding heart.

Tessa could feel them releasing her wrists. Twin sets of hands massaged their way down over her arms, working out any stiffness. There was none. Her body was like pudding, limp and relaxed.

Her ankles and legs received the same treatment. When their hands met at the tops of her thighs, they both slid a finger up her pussy. The small touch made her grumble and twist away, still too sensitive there to be teased.

They abandoned her tender flesh, but her relief was only momentary. Tessa groaned, annoyed at being disturbed as they lifted off the bed. The feel of a hard, hot male body sliding beneath her warned her that the disturbance was just beginning.

The long, thick erection poking into her butt made her murmur a half-hearted protest. Expecting that cock to nudge against her back entrance, she was surprised when they levered her up, over and down the steel hard length till her pussy felt overfilled and stretched to its limits.

Tessa groaned again, this time with renewed desire. Her hips arched, flexed, attempting to take in more of him, take him deeper. Strong hands bit into her hips, stilling her motions.

Before she could voice a complaint, a mouth burrowed into the smooth flesh of her naked cunt. His tongue flicked out, sliding down the length of her slit, savoring the warm, musky flavor of her desire.

She gasped at his first tentative foray, squirming away from him and making Ty moan. Chase grinned at the results. She could squirm all she wanted. She wasn't going anywhere.

With her legs held by Ty, Tessa was completely open, totally vulnerable for his feasting and she tasted delicious. He trailed his tongue down her pussy again, enjoying her flavor as he worked his way back up to her distended little bud. Pulling her clit with his lips earned him another moan, echoed again by Ty.

Tessa's eye blinked open, staring into the darkness of the blindfold as Chase worked her sensitive bud. It was unlike anything she had ever experienced, being packed so full of cock while a wicked tongue worked over her tender clit.

The buildup inside her pussy, the tight winding of tension, threatened to whip free an orgasm that made the previous one look like a momentary blip, a flash-fire in the face of a volcano. His tongue slid down to her parted lips and licked around where Ty and her were joined.

Tessa couldn't breathe for the pleasure ripping her body to shreds with its gagged claws. Her inner muscles gripped the shaft buried deep in her, pulsing over its hard length for endlessly long seconds as her orgasm contracted every muscle in her body. Chase's tongue tormented her painfully sensitive flesh, refusing to allow her climax to end.

"Please!" Tessa sobbed.

She needed a minute, just one or her heart was going to explode. There was no way her lungs could keep pace with it as fast as it was racing. Her chest ached painfully and she needed to calm down.

"I think she's had enough, Chase," Ty growled. He certainly had. If Chase didn't let up, he wasn't going to last to the final act.

"Yes! Yes. Yes," Tessa babbled. "A moment, I can't breathe."

"Hmm." Chase lifted his head. "Pity, I was enjoying myself."

"Please, I..." Tessa gasped.

"It's all right, baby," Ty murmured as Chase rolled off her. "We've got you."

Chapter 19

Tessa groaned as Ty's cock slid out of her, stroking across her oversensitive muscles. Warm, hard bodies settled down on either side of her. As usual, they crowded into her. It felt good here, safe. Tessa didn't have it left in her to fight. She barely had the strength to snuggle into the man on her right.

"Tired, baby?" Chase nuzzled her neck from behind. Tessa instinctively rolled her head, exposing more of her flesh to his mouth.

"Mm-hmm."

"Feel good?"

The hand Ty had resting on her hip began to draw circles on her sensitive skin. It tickled and she shifted slightly to let him know to stop. Instead, his touch grew firmer, more sensual.

"Baby?" Ty prodded her.

"What?" Tessa mumbled, annoyed at being held back from sleep.

"You enjoyed what we did, didn't you?"

"You know I did."

Tessa rolled away from Ty, trying to escape his wandering hand. She found herself snuggled into Chase's arms with Ty's hand still caressing closer and closer to her pussy.

"You wouldn't let anybody else do the things we do to you, would you, Tessa?" Chase was just as talkative as Ty.

"Mm-mm."

"Is that a no?"

"No."

"You know why that is, baby?"

Ty's hand made it to her wet folds, rubbing circles against the newly bared skin. It was most distracting. Her pussy still tingled with the aftereffects of her recent releases. As good as his touch felt, there were small sizzling shards of pain mixed with the pleasure. Her poor flesh had been overworked. It needed a break, just like the rest of her. Tessa squirmed in a futile attempt to dislodge his hand. When that failed, she tried a more direct approach.

"Sleep now."

"Not till you answer us."

"What?"

"You trust us, don't you, baby?" Ty whispered against the back of her ear.

"Yes."

"You love us," Chase stated against her lips.

"Yes."

No sooner, had the words left her mouth then he was kissing her. It was a kiss of absolute possession. So heated and demanding, it made it clear that she was not going to be getting to sleep anytime soon.

Chase was relentless, rolling his head from one angle to another as he tested their fit, searching for the position that would allow him the deepest penetration. Ty wasn't content to play the part of voyeur. His fingers slid down her pussy, his thumb stopping over her clit, applying subtle pressure while two fingers moved lower to her weeping opening.

Tessa broke her kiss with Chase as Ty's thick fingers filled her, scissoring to stretch her wide. She only managed to get a single gasp of breath before Ty's lips covered hers. His tongue was sweet, his taste a mixture of man and lust, wildly, deliciously addictive. As he plundered her mouth, his fingers began fucking into her pulsing channel with growing ferocity. It was too much. Her body, still alive with the aftershocks of her previous climaxes, burst again.

Ty swallowed her scream, driving her orgasm higher as he continued to toy with her pussy. Chase added to the sensation, kissing his way down her chest, rubbing his stubbled cheek into her breasts, rasping her tender nipples with his coarse hair and then soothing the ache with soft licks of his tongue. It was a voluptuous mixture of textures and pleasures.

Her body was on fire, any second she would start smoking, burst into flames and burn her lovers. It would serve them right for forcing such excessive ecstasy on her.

Ty could feel her body trembling out of control and knew she wouldn't last much longer. He, for one, wanted to ride her into her last release, to take his own before she passed out.

Blindly reaching over his shoulder, he fumbled for the lubricant he had left on the nightstand. He felt Chase's chin nudge his hand and he abandoned the position to turn and find the lube.

Chase delighted at her groan, at the hands that twined in his hair and tried to pull him away from her cunt. Tessa had a low tolerance for pleasure. It was one of the things he loved about her, how quickly she came for them. He knew they were pushing her further than they ever had. It was only the beginning. In the days, weeks, years to come they would stretch her boundaries, take her to entirely new heights and realms.

He felt Ty lifting her, turning her on her side so he could access her luscious ass. Inadvertently, Ty pushed her pussy right into Chase's waiting mouth. Showing the same lack of mercy he had earlier, Chase devoured her sweet flesh. Above him, Tessa moaned and begged, her hands gripping his hair painfully as her hips arched into his tongue.

When she thought she could bear no more, one, then two, then three thick fingers invaded her ass. She arched away from the pleasurable pressure of being stretched. There was no escape. A quick, clever tongue greeted her on the other side. It twirled over her over sensitized clit, making the little bud send out conflicting vibrations of pain and pleasure.

With a strength she did not know she had, she ripped Chase from her pussy. Gasping in massive quantities of air, Tessa fought to find some anchor in a world that was being obliterated by extreme sensations.

If she thought she was getting a reprieve, she realized her error a moment later when Chase lifted her thigh over his. He slid between her legs. The hard, rounded head of his cock pushed against her pussy.

With one solid thrust, he impaled her on his overgrown erection. Her sheath was made tighter by their position, by her inability to spread her other leg. It made his already large cock feel enormous. Instinctively her leg lifted, climbing over his hip, trying to compensate for the lack of space.

Even as she managed to spread herself a little wider, she felt Ty's rough hands pulling her ass cheeks wide, felt the bulbous head of his cock pressing into her. Tessa bit her lip, her head thrashing back and forth as he slowly forged into her ass.

"Oh, God!"

There wasn't enough room for them both, not in this position and she felt stretched beyond her capacity. The pressure was so intense it was almost too painful.

Then they began to thrust. Slowly at first, alternating strokes, but quickly their tempo sped up. Faster, harder, in unison they fucked into her, unleashing the primal animal within her.

She snarled and bucked, scratching Chase as she rode the storm they had ignited within her. Ty dug his fingers into her hips, trying to bring rhythm into her mindless thrashing. The feel of her tight ass squeezing along his length was almost enough to make him lose control. Then her climax exploded onto a whole new level.

She screamed as she arched backward, slamming her ass down along his length, and Ty could contain his pleasure no more. Every muscle in his body contracted and expanded, convulsing as his semen seared its way through his cock and flooded her ass.

Chase heard his roar of fulfillment echoed and knew Ty had just found his release. Chase's climax felt never ending as Tessa's pussy milked his length with pulses too fast to register. Between Ty's cock pushing down from behind and the tightness of Tessa's sheath, it felt like a velvet-lined steel fist was trying to squeeze his cock out of existence. He bit down on her shoulder, pumping into her as hard and long as he could, until he was completely drained and his cock gave up the battle. He collapsed onto the bed as the rest of his body followed his dick and went flaccid.

He barely had enough strength to pull out of Tessa's still-pulsing cunt and wrap an arm around her. She murmured a complaint, her hot breath feeling like a cool breeze against the overheated skin on his chest.

"Do you love me, Tessa?" Chase wanted to hear her say it again, needed to hear it.

"Sleep." She barely managed to form the word.

"Tell us you love us, Tessa," Ty prodded, molding himself to her back.

"Love you."

Tessa passed into the dark world of unconsciousness even as the words fell from her lips. The world went black as her body went limp, but even through the abyss she could hear their whispers.

"I love you, too, baby girl," Chase said. "You're my heart and soul."

"I love you," Ty breathed over her ear. "I can't breathe without you, can't live without you. You have all of me, my love."

Tessa smiled. It was a sweet dream.

Chapter 20

The warm sunlight heated her cheeks and brightened the darkness behind her lids. Tessa sighed, not wanting to open her eyes and face the new day. Burying her head deeper into her pillow, she inhaled the erotic mixture of sex and men.

Ty and Chase. They'd awakened her early. Too early. The sun's light had barely begun to brighten the sky behind her curtains. She'd been tired, grumpy and sore. They hadn't cared.

Oh, they'd started with the excuse of massaging her. Hard, warm hands rubbing up and down her body had quickly turned to soft lips, wet licks and sharp nips. Soon enough their attention had narrowed to focus on her most sensitive places. Breasts, pussy, the tender skin at the small of her back, the sweet spot in the crook of her neck — when it came to them, there wasn't much of her body that wasn't sensitive to their touch.

Only when they had her moaning and begging had they finally taken her. Separately, together, on her back, face down, on all fours; they'd maneuvered her into one position after another in their insatiable drive for more.

The fuzzy memory of talking to Marcie popped into her head. Tessa frowned as she tried to recall the details. She had talked to Marcie on the phone, telling her she wasn't coming in to work today.

The problem was, she didn't remember calling Marcie. She had a vague memory of a phone ringing. The longer she concentrated on that fact, the more her memories congealed into one, smooth-flowing, highly embarrassing event.

Marcie had called. Ty had answered the phone because she'd been busy being ridden by Chase. She guessed Marcie had been distressed by the sound of Tessa screaming in the background, because Ty had thrust the phone to the side of her face and ordered her to tell Marcie she was all right.

Tessa had barely been capable of coherent words, much less complete sentences. Somehow, though, she'd managed to grunt out enough single syllable words to appease Marcie. More likely Marcie had accurately guessed what Tessa was going to be spending the day doing.

Tessa groaned and buried her face deeper into the pillow. Marcie would never let her live that down, not for a moment.

She's going to be mad enough about Jace. That thought made her frown. Yes, She had sold out Marcie and agreed to set her up on a blind date with Jace. Why had she done that?

Ty. Tyler. Tyler Banning. Banning & Dunn. Oh, shit!

As the memories of the morning repeated, memories of the past night were added and things became crystal clear. They had broken into her apartment, used her physical weakness for them to trick her into confessing her feelings.

"Sleeping Beauty awakes."

Chase's comment had her head snapping around in surprise. He was leaning against the doorframe to the living room, dressed in nothing but a pair of faded blue button-flies. He looked like he'd walked right out of the pages of a magazine, all rippling abs, bulging biceps, rugged jaw and sleep-tussled hair.

Though she was mad at him, her body was so far under his sexual spell that she could feel her pussy cream, her nipples pucker. Anticipation at him taking off those jeans and joining her in bed heated her entire body.

"What are you doing here?" She tried to sound mad, but her throat was sore from all the screaming she'd done the night before. The hoarse tone made her words seem desperate, scared even. She compensated by glaring at him.

"Where else would I be?"

"I don't know." Tessa shrugged with a nonchalance she didn't feel. "Off screwing over another innocent woman?"

"I thought we settled this last night, Tessa." Chase shoved off the doorframe, strolling into the room with a casualness she didn't trust. She could sense the predatory intent in him.

"All that was settled last night was that you two are bigger assholes than I originally suspected."

"We confess our love to you and that makes us assholes?" Chase quirked a brow at her. "Baby, you're crazier than I thought."

"Don't expect me to believe your lies," Tessa snapped. "I'm not sure what angle you're playing, but I'll figure it out."

"I should tan your ass for saying that."

"You wouldn't dare." Tessa's eyes narrowed on him, reading the slight tensing of his body. When he pounced, she lunged toward the left side of the bed and almost made it off in time. Almost.

He caught her by the thigh with one strong hand. His other settled on her hip to hold her down and in place. Tessa ended up in the embarrassing, and alarming, position of being ass up, the lower half of her body still on the bed while the rest of her was bent over the side. Her forehead thumped on the hard wood floors as she stretched her arms out in the vain attempt to pull herself out from under him and the rest of the way off the bed.

"Be still!"

Chase shifted. Expecting him to spank her, he shocked a squeal out of her by raking his teeth down the globe of one ass cheek and biting her soft flesh. Tessa felt the stinging pain vibrate into a cascade of pleasure, drenching her in a warm glow. That didn't stop her from being pissed, it only added to it.

"You bit me!" Tessa flailed about, trying desperately to escape.

He did again. This time, his tongue slipped out to softly lick the wound, turning Tessa's scream into a groan. That devilish tongue continued tasting her, working its way down her ass toward the seam that divided one leg from the other.

"No. No. No," Tessa babbled, but, as usual, he ignored her.

With his normal sense of entitlement, Chase shoved his face right into her pussy using his hands on her hips to angle her up for better access. Tessa knew she should fight him, should do whatever was necessary to escape him before he once more reduced her to a quivering mass of spinelessness that was willing to do or say whatever he wanted.

God help her, it was what she wanted, too. She wanted it all. Wanted his mouth on her, eating at her with greedy, carnal abandon. Wanted his hands touching her, sliding over her with their possessive strength. Wanted his cock, riding her through one orgasm and into the next. Damn her traitorous body, but she wanted that the most of all.

She clenched her teeth and fought the delirious pleasure he was forcing on her, trying to maintain her will and retain her shattered dignity.

Damn it, I'm not going to come! That was her last thought before her climax erupted through her with savage force, ripping through her with such speed she was terrified her muscles would splinter from the pressure.

She sobbed Chase's name and again her hands pulled futilely on the floor, trying to escape the soul-stealing ecstasy. Chase growled against her flesh, the small vibrations igniting a cascade of sparkling pleasure. His hands bit into her skin, holding her still as he fed on her cunt like some starved and desperate animal.

Chase yanked her backward and further onto his tongue. It was in as far as he could go, but her tight sheath tried to suction him deeper as another wave of hot cream flooded his mouth.

Delicious.

That was the only way to describe the taste of her sweet, honeyed fluids. He could dine on her for hours, had done so and would never grow tired of it. Now, though, his cock was demanding to be freed. The tyrant wanted its turn with Tessa's tight little cunt. Chase's hands ripped open the buttons holding back his erection. With quick motions, he lifted her up further and slid his knees between her splayed tights. He rubbed his cock into her wet folds until his length was coated in her slick desire. It was all he could do not to slam into her.

"Tell me this is what you want," he demanded.

"Please, Chase."

"Tell me!"

"Oh, God, yes. Please, please, I ache." Tessa knew she was begging, but didn't care. If he didn't fill her soon, she would go out of her mind.

"And you love me, don't you?"

"Chase!"

"Don't you?"

"Yes, damn you!"

He needed no further encouragement. He yanked her backward and hard down onto his length. Heedless of the raw cries spilling helplessly from her throat, Chase began to pump himself mercilessly into her. With hard, plunging strokes, he stretched the tight, heated walls of her pussy with ruthless intent.

The delicious burn of her muscles expanding to take his blunt, heavy shaft had colors dancing behind her closed lids as her world exploded in sensation. In a blinding flash of white-hot flames, she came.

Chase felt her sheath contract around his length. The ferocious squeezing was nearly painful and his lips pulled back in a snarl as he shafted her harder, deeper. Then he heard her scream his name and the steel control holding back his own release broke.

It had never been like this with any other woman. This was not the simple matter of pleasure of the flesh, of a basic release of sexual need, but a matter of the heart.

Chase wanted to possess more than just Tessa's body. He wanted ownership of her heart, of her very soul. Every time he took her into his arms, he gained a little more of those two precious commodities. And he lost a little bit more of his own.

Chapter 21

"I hate you," Tessa mumbled into Chase's chest even as she contradicted the statement by snuggling in closer to his warmth. Not awake an hour and already she needed another nap. At this rate, she would be lucky to get out of bed by the end of the week.

"You love me," Chase countered, completely relaxed.

"I don't want to."

"That's too damn bad, because I love you and I'm not letting go." As if to emphasize his point, his arm tightened around her.

"Yeah? For how long?"

"Forever."

"Oh, please. I know all about you, Chase." Tessa sighed. The conversation was ruining her enjoyment in being held by him. She tried to shrug his arm away, but he held tight.

"Good, then you know I love you."

"Along with hundreds of others."

"What the hell does that mean?"

"I read all about your addiction to variety. What do you try to do? Fit the entire alphabet into one week?"

"All in the past." Chase dismissed her concerns. "Besides, I don't think you can complain about my experience when you're reaping the benefits of it."

"You really are a bastard, you know that?"

"Yeah, but you still love me."

"Stop saying that!"

"Why? It's true and I love you. See how neatly that all works out?"

"I'm going to figure out a way to stop caring about you."

"That's going to be kind of hard to do while being married to me."

Tessa gasped. "Married? I'm not going to marry you!"

"Of course you are, baby." Chase stretched and grabbed something off the nightstand. "I got your ring right here."

"My ri– " The word died in her mouth as her breathing came to a screeching halt. Her eyes stared at the small jewelers box until her vision blurred as her eyes filled with tears. She knew that box, knew it because she had made Marcie dye it that special shade of brown.

My lady has the most enchanting hazel eyes. They darken with her love for me and I would like the ring box to match.

Chase? Chase was Michael, the mysterious, wealthy client? But he had ordered the rings the day after she met them. That meant... All the arguments and justifications she had erected to keep Chase and Ty at bay began to shred as her mind whirled with the ramifications.

Chase was startled when Tessa burst into tears. It was the last reaction he had anticipated. From happiness to anger, nothing could have shocked him more. The gut-wrenching sobs didn't sound a thing like tears of joy. They sounded more like abject grief.

Completely at a loss, Chase pulled Tessa on top of him and held her tightly. In the tradition of helpless men everywhere, he murmured inconsequential assurances while rubbing her back. It didn't appear to help.

Tessa seemed completely unaware of him. As her heaving breath broke her sobs into ragged gasps, she began to babble. At first her words were incoherent, disjointed rambles that Chase didn't understand.

Tessa managed to vocalize a complete thought. "This is all wrong. It's wrong."

"What's wrong, baby?" Chase asked absently, more focused on trying to get her to calm down than what she as saying.

"You, me, this. It's all wrong."

"Don't worry, baby," Chase assured her. "I love you and I'm going to take good care of you."

"But that's what's wrong!"

"I'm not understanding, Tessa. What exactly is wrong?"

"You shouldn't love me, don't you see that!"

"What the hell are you talking about now? Jesus, woman, will you make sense for once?"

"Don't you see, Chase?" Tessa lifted her head. Her bloodshot eyes, dripping with tears, implored him to understand. "I'm not the right type of woman for you. You belong with one of those models you normally date, the high-society sophisticates that know how to handle themselves socially and never have a hair out of place."

Chase's eyes narrowed with her words. He felt the fine prickles of his temper starting to ignite. It was a rare event when he got mad, but as he listened to Tessa continue to speak, there was no disguising the heat boiling through his blood.

"I'm not like that. I don't know what fork goes with what dish if there is more than one. Hell, I'm not even sure how to set a table properly," Tessa continued, completely unaware of the way Chase tensed beneath her. "I iron but within a half hour, my clothes are always rumpled and wrinkled. I could brush my hair all day long and it would still knot. I'm short and fat and all I'll do is embarra—"

Tessa's sentence ended in a scream as Chase's palm came down hard on her ass. The stinging blow was not one of the playful slaps he normally gave her. It jarred her out of her self-pity long enough to glare at him.

"That hurt!"

"It was supposed to. If I ever hear you talk about yourself that way again, I'll blister your ass so bad you wouldn't be able to sit for a whole week!"

"I'm just telling the truth!"

Tessa's indignant glare dissolved into a shocked expression as he spanked her again, harder this time. She began to fight his hold. Chase wasn't about to let her go. Wrapping his legs around hers, he used his arms to pin hers to her sides.

"Now you listen to me, Tessa, and you listen good," Chase commanded when he had her pinned. "I love you, everything about you. I don't care about forks or table settings. If you're worried about wrinkled clothes, go naked. I like you best that way.

"I love your body and all your curves. You are the most beautiful, exciting woman I've ever been with. Hell, I can't get enough of you. Do you honestly think I can go for hours with just any woman? Because I can't. That's you, baby, what you do to me."

"What about if I get pregnant?" Tessa demanded, not knowing the delight her words sent through him. "When I'm too big to stand without help? You still going to think I'm beautiful and exciting?"

"Hell, yeah! Just the idea makes me hard. Feel." He shifted, pressing his erection into her.

"What if we can't have sex? If the doctor forbids it?"

"Then I'll wear out that ass of yours. When the doctor forbids that," Chase continued when she opened her mouth to object, "I'm going to spread your legs and bury my head between your thighs and eat that delicious cunt of yours, make you suck my cock at the same time."

Tessa pursed her lips and studied him for a moment.

"You're not going to be reasonable about this, are you?"

"You're the one who's being unreasonable."

"I guess we're at a draw then."

"I guess so."

"Then what are we going to do?"

Chase reached for the ring box he had dropped on the bed and flicked it open. He struggled with her to get her hand, but in the end his superior strength won out and he managed to slide the ring onto her finger.

"You're going to marry Ty and me."

"I hate to break it to you, but that's a tiny bit illegal."

"You'll be married to Ty legally here in the States. Then we're going to rent a private yacht, go out to sea and have a ceremony where you're wed to both of us."

"You've got this all figured out."

"I do." Chase gave her a smile, letting his hand caress the luscious curve of her ass. "So why don't you just relax and let us take care of everything?"

Tessa sighed and admitted defeat. There was no stopping Chase, that much was obvious, and she didn't have the heart to try anymore. He was offering her the fairy tale. As much as her rational side told her to be wary and cautious, her heart only had so much resistance in it.

Her thoughts coalesced around a single thought. She lifted her face to Chase. The look of sleepy contentment on his face gave her pause.

Still, she wondered…

"Chase?"

"Hmm." He didn't even bother to open his eyes.

"Where is Ty?"

"Ty." Chase blinked for a moment, clearly caught off guard by the question. It fed a moment of apprehension that struck Tessa and was not alleviated by Chase's evasive answer.

"He had to take care of a few things."

"Things," Tessa repeated, her mind immediately jumping to the image of one beautiful, blond thing Ty might be taking care of.

"What?" Chase frowned down at her.

"Olivia?" Tessa hated herself for even saying it, but could not control her need to know.

"Olivia." Chase snorted. "Nah, nothing like that. He had to go take care of a few mundane business matters."

"Business." Tessa repeated doubtfully.

"Yeah, you know, like checking the mail for bills."

"Bills." Now Tessa knew he was lying.

"Yeah, grab the newspaper before the neighbors steal it."

"Newspaper." Tessa's eyes widened. Her mind immediately jumped to just what was in the day's papers. *Oh, shit!*

Chase appeared unaware of the sudden change in Tessa's demeanor. He continued to rattle off a variety of daily tasks that Ty had to see to, only stopping when Tessa sat up abruptly.

"I gotta..." Tessa searched her mind for a good excuse, but it was too late. A second after she swung her legs over the edge of the bed, the back door banged open.

"*Tessa!*"

Ty was home.

Chapter 22

"I need a shower."

Tessa threw that desperate excuse at Chase as she bolted for the bathroom. She managed to evade Chase's arms, slamming the door as Ty came charging into the room. Chase's eyes cut from the bathroom door to his partner and widened in alarm.

He couldn't remember the last time he'd seen Ty so upset. Not even when he had been arrested the previous night had he appeared this unhinged. Ty immediately moved to the bathroom door and began beating on it, roaring Tessa's name. The only response was the sound of the shower turning on.

"I know you can hear me!"

Chase rolled his eyes at that. People five miles away could probably hear him.

"What has you worked into a lather?"

Ty scowled and stepped back from the solid wood door. His only response was to throw the section of newspaper he'd wadded up in his fist at Chase. It took a moment for Chase to smooth out the wrinkles so he could see it, but when he did, his eyes were immediately caught on the picture and the headline covering the front page of the local business section.

Prominent, Respected Businessman Arrested For Prostitution. Right beside the bold-face type was a picture of Ty's booking shot. Chase had to school his features to keep the grin from breaking through. This was classic, definitely one to be matted and framed for the office wall.

When he was sure he could keep the amusement out of his tone, Chase looked back at Ty, who had returned to beating on the bathroom door.

"You're going to have to come out of there sometime!"

There was no response from the bathroom to that threat. Ty turned his anger on chase. "Do you see what she did?"

"Ah, well, I hate to inject reason into this, but you weren't arrested till you confessed," Chase pointed out diplomatically.

From the narrowing of his eyes, Ty was not in the mood for diplomacy or reason. "Third paragraph down," he said.

"What?"

Ty wasn't paying him any attention. He renewed his efforts to beat down the door. Chase counted down to the third paragraph in the article. As he read, his eyes widened. This time he couldn't hold back the grin. Their Tessa had a few more teeth and a lot worse bite than he had given her credit for.

> One of Tyler Banning's former clients, speaking on the condition of anonymity, expressed disappointment in the services rendered. "For a man in his profession, I was amazed at his inexperience. I would definitely not seek his services again."

The sound of the bathroom door splintering and the high-pitched shriek that immediately followed drew Chase's attention to the now-broken door. He cocked his head as he listened to the argument that raged to life in the bathroom.

Bless her spirit, it didn't matter how wrong Tessa was, she was matching Ty shout for shout, accusation for accusation. Tessa's shouts took on a desperate, huskier tone as she begged Ty to stop. She pleaded with Ty not to do something and Chase had to wonder what all that was about.

Unable to deny his curiosity, he rolled out of bed as the first distinctive crack changed Tessa's words into an incoherent scream, a mixture of pleasure and pain, of excitement and apprehension. The charged air leaking out of the bathroom was shattered by two more loud smacks as Tessa's screams turned into moans.

Chase paused in the remains of the door to take in the erotic sight of the man he loved like a brother disciplining the woman he would love beyond a single lifetime. Tessa was bent over at the waist, her face plastered against the tile wall, her full lips parted as she moaned out her rising pleasure.

Ty stood behind her, his cock shoved halfway up her ass as he delivered another sharp slap to her already reddened rear cheeks. Tessa groaned out her approval for the discipline as her hips arched, blindly seeking more.

She needed it, needed him to ride her with the rough urgency his savage treatment was inspiring in her body. Her pussy ached and wept with the need to be filled. Her ass tightened possessively around the cock stretching it, unwilling to relinquish the right to be ridden by the hard shaft.

Ty delivered another smack to her ass. These were no love taps. Like Chase's spankings earlier, they were hard blows that made her ass tighten painfully around the steel pole lodged in her ass. The pleasure bloomed outward, making her clit tingle and her nipples pucker.

"Please," Tessa moaned, mindlessly.

"Please, what?" Ty growled, slapping her ass again.

He kept his own groan locked behind clenched jaws as he felt her tighten around him. It was heaven and hell to be buried in the vise of her ass. His hardened flesh screamed at him to move, to lend friction to the pressure, to pump himself into her until ecstasy rained a sweet release down over them.

"Ty!" Tessa squealed when he hit her even harder.

"Tell me what you want," Ty demanded.

"Fuck me! I want you to fuck my ass!"

"I thought you weren't going to seek my services again."

"Please, Ty."

"You told the whole town how disappointed you were in my experience," Ty pushed, angered anew as he repeated her comments.

"Damn it, Ty! I was mad and I had a right to be."

Wrong answer, babe, Chase thought as Ty yanked Tessa upright, impaling his full length into her ass. The motion had her crying out, writhing in Ty's arms. Chase's cock pulsed with demand, urging him to step up and fill the empty cunt that now belonged to him.

He knew better. Ty was riled up enough. He did not want to get in the middle. It was Ty's right to handle this matter on his own. Tessa's scream broke Chase's concentration and he watched with heated eyes as Ty delivered another openhanded slap, this one to her pussy.

"Are you still disappointed in me, Tessa?" Ty asked, fighting his own desires back.

"Yes!" Tessa snapped. "I want you to fu—"

Her demand ended in another scream as fire shot through her clit. Her entire body contracted with the first ripple of climax. She panted through the extreme pleasure. Just one more slap would break the tense bands holding the bliss at bay.

"Again."

"What was that, baby? Again? Or never again?"

"Damn it, Ty!"

Tessa struggled against his hold. The movement heightened the pressure coming from her ass, intensifying the pleasure but not releasing her from the sharp claws of denied ecstasy.

"You know what men like me do to people who publicly slander and defame us?"

"Fuck them raw?"

"Sue," Ty corrected.

"Fine, sue me. But first, fuck me. Please, Ty. I need you." If she thought that declaration was going to save her, she was sadly mistaken.

"Tomorrow I'm going to call my lawyer and find out how much I would get out of a suit."

"You're kidding!" Tessa gasped, wiggling anew.

"Be still!" Ty slapped her pussy again, making sure her clit took most of the impact. She mewed under the force of the blow, panting with her need.

"Are you listening to me?"

"Yes," Tessa panted.

"My lawyer will probably want restitution in the millions."

"Millions?" Tessa swallowed hard. "I don't have that kind of money."

"You can work it off."

"I can?"

"With your legs spread. You'll be my personal slave." Ty's cock pulsed at his words, loving the sound of that. "Mine to do with what I want, when I want, wherever and however I want. Understand?"

"That's insane!"

Tessa screamed and shuddered as he delivered another smartly placed slap to her cunt, causing her clit to beacon red-hot shards of rapture through her body and leaving her, again, on the verge of orgasm.

"Understand?"

"Yes." Tessa would do anything, say anything, to end this torment.

"We're going to have to set a dollar amount on your services. How about you show me your skills and I'll tell you what I think they're worth."

Before Tessa could respond to that inflammatory statement, Ty bent her back over and began thrusting. All thoughts, concerns fled with the feel of his long, heated shaft powering in and out of her ass. In seconds, she was moaning, arching into his thrusts, needing to feel him harder, deeper.

Ty felt Tessa's muscles pinching down on him, could hear the ragged tempo of her breathing increase as she approached her climax. It wasn't good enough. He wanted to brand her with a release that seared his name, his touch onto her very soul.

Reaching around, he slid his finger over the smooth, silky skin of her mound. Searching for the tender nub hidden at the top of her folds, he pressed down over the sensitive bud so every stroke of his cock was matched by her clit rubbing against his calloused fingertip.

That little addition of pleasure sent Tessa off the edge of the cliff and into the mind-shattering rhapsody. She screamed out her release, thrashing beneath the onslaught of a pleasure too great for her body to contain.

Ty felt her muscles clamp down the moment her climax hit her. Icy shards of pleasure contrasted sharply with the eruption of hot seed that shot from his balls, down his cock and flooded her body as he found his own release.

He came for what felt like an eternity as his soul tried to force its way through his body, making him glow and burn with the magnitude of his own climax. Then in a blink, it was gone, leaving him weak but content.

Chapter 23

"If you two don't mind, I'd like to get a shower."

Ty cut Chase a hard look, but made no comment as he pulled his dick out of Tessa's ass. Silently, he cleaned Tessa and himself off before lifting her into his arms.

Chase understood the determined look in Ty's eyes as he brushed past him. He was not done with Tessa. Tessa was obviously ignorant of what was coming her way. Her eyes were closed, her head resting trustingly on Ty's shoulder. She looked half asleep already.

"The water's cold!" Chase yelled as he stepped into the stall.

"Tough shit," Ty tossed back.

He didn't care if Chase had to take a cold shower, or even if he took one at all. All he cared about was the woman in his arms. The engagement ring Chase had picked up from Marcie that morning caught in the sunlight as he lowered her onto the bed.

Chase had put his ring on her right hand, leaving her left for Ty. The sight both pleased and annoyed him. He wanted his ring on her finger. She was going to be married to him as far as polite society was concerned. Snatching the second ring box off the nightstand, he lifted her left hand.

When he had his ring on her finger, he sat back. That was better, but it didn't ease the ache in his heart. It had been there since he read the article in the paper. That had ignited his temper, but it was not the demon driving him. It was her biting comments. Even if they had been given in the heat of anger, they had cut him to the quick.

The pain scorched him and every time he thought about her quote, his anger reignited. His heart was exposed, vulnerable and he hated it. She had done this to him. He'd been right to avoid emotional attachment, but it was too late now. He was hers and, by God, she was his.

In a heartbeat, his cock went from half-mast to fully raised. There was no reason to deprive himself. Ty pulled Tessa further down the bed, spreading her legs while she slept, completely unaware of her fate. She did murmur, a slight sound of disapproval when he dipped his fingers into her cunt and assured himself she was more than wet enough to take him.

Kneeling between her splayed legs, he lifted her by the hips and roughly yanked her down his erection. Tessa's eyes flew wide open. Her gasp turned into a groan as he unceremoniously began to pound into her.

She was so tight. No matter how many times they took her, no matter how juicy her pussy was, he always had to fight for every inch his cock claimed. He could feel every tiny stretch of muscle, every ripple as her sheath danced with excitement, sucking at him with amazing strength.

His balls tightened painfully at the teasing motions of her pussy, his cock hardening, lengthening that final inch that only she pulled out of him. A flame of intense arousal blistered through Ty, warning an early release was imminent. Holding tightly to the reigns of his own control, he plundered her tight pussy.

Tessa was given no choice but to ride out the storm of passion that erupted through her tired body. He looped her knees over his elbows and leaned forward, impaling her with his full length.

He held nothing back, possessing her cunt with each forceful invasion. She was helpless in his grip, unable to do deny him the response he pulled from her with each stroke of his cock. He was big, so thick, so full inside her, causing the most delicious sensations to ripple up her sheath, over her clit and outward to where her toes curled and her fingers bit into the sheets.

Reality faded, ceasing to exist as Tessa's world narrowed to this one moment. There was nothing else, just the feel of Ty buried deep inside her, fucking into her with hard-driving strokes.

His pace quickened, his strength increasing until they were both grunting, striving for the ultimate culmination. Beneath them, the bed shook, rattled, bouncing against the wall so hard the night table trembled and the lamp fell over, the ceramic base shattering on the floor.

Neither of them cared, barely noticing. The band binding Tessa to the world of physical reality snapped, boomeranging her into a universe filled only with intense, shattering explosions of ecstasy. Ty followed her, slamming his cock one last time into the pulsing depths of her pussy.

They fell back to the real world in a heap. Flushed, breathing hard, their sweat-slicked bodies suctioned together as they fought to regain control of their racing hearts. Several minutes passed as Ty rested his head against her breasts. Idly, her hand stroked through his hair. The gentle caress lulled him into wanting to stay there, like that, forever.

Tessa's mind was racing, something was missing. As hot and wild as the sex had been, it had lacked the tenderness underneath that made what they had so special. She wanted that sweetness back, but felt at a loss as to how to get it.

The glint of the ring on her finger caught her attention. It was the second one she had made, Ty's ring, and he must have put it on her when she had fallen asleep. Staring at the beautiful emerald, it clicked.

It wasn't anger driving him ruthlessly. That wasn't what was motivating him. It was merely his defense, the same as hers had been yesterday. He was hurt, perhaps even a little insecure. Her comments about his lack of ability must have hit more than a nerve. The shot must have embedded itself straight in his heart.

Yesterday, when she had given her quote, she had been focused on her own pain and anger. It was no excuse. She had done wrong, but fucking her to death wasn't going to make it right.

As if reading the direction of her thoughts, Ty lifted his head. His dark, hooded gaze met hers and she could see then quite clearly what he was trying to hide. It made her want to soothe him and tell him everything would be all right, but that probably wouldn't go over well.

"Ready to go again?" he asked.

Stretching up she gave him a tender, chaste kiss. "I love you Ty. Chase and you make me feel things that I've never felt before. Give me pleasures I never even knew existed. When I found out you had lied to me, I felt so hurt and betrayed. Those feelings were even stronger because of the love I have for you. Can you understand that?"

Something flickered in his eyes as he slowly nodded.

"I shouldn't have done the things I did, said the things I said, but I wanted to hurt you. It was wrong and I'm sorry. Can't you forgive me?"

"I guess I can try," Ty allowed slowly. He sounded begrudging, but she could see the softening in his eyes.

"I hope so. I'd be proud to be your wife, happy to be your servant. Either way, I'll love you for the rest of my life. Now, if you want to go another round, I'm ready."

Ty stared at her from under his lashes for a moment before one side of his lips quirked up.

"You're sneaky."

"Thank you."

"You're off the hook for now, but I meant what I said, you're going to work off the rest." Ty smiled for the first time since entering the apartment. "I got your room all ready."

"I'm not sure I want to know." Tessa studied that smile with concern.

"Oh, but I want to tell you."

"Ty—"

"I have harnesses, an examination table, hooks, chains, floggers, leather and velvet, lots of toys, and a bed. A very big bed, of course."

"Of course," Tessa paused, before her curiosity got the better of her. "An examination table?"

"Ever played doctor?" Ty's grin took a lecherous turn.

"Never mind," Tessa interjected. "Forget I asked."

"The game has gotten a little more grown-up and a whole lot more fun," Ty teased.

"Can I at least get some sleep, first?"

"Course you can." Ty settled down beside her, pulling her into his arms. "You get some rest."

"Hmm."

Tessa cuddled up next to him. In less than a minute she was asleep. Ty smiled and pulled the blanket up to haphazardly tuck it around them. This was perfect, just the way he wanted things to be.

That fact still scared him slightly. He was operating without a map, without a plan. For the rest of his life he was going to be operating in a world dominated by two of the most insane people he knew, Tessa and Chase.

They both had the ability to hurt him, but he didn't have the will to leave. He loved Tessa, needed her, and couldn't imagine his life without Chase in it. Yep, he was doomed.

The sound of Chase coming back into the room drew his head up.

Chase arched a brow. "Get it out of your system?"

"For the moment." Ty thought about the playroom that was waiting back at his house. "You want to pack some bags for her?"

"Why don't you?" Chase shot back. "And I'll keep our lovely company in the bed."

"We're going to have to figure a way to make this work."

"It will sort itself out." Chase knew Ty was no longer talking about Tessa's bags. He was worrying over the future and how the two friends were actually going to handle sharing a woman on a permanent basis.

"I hope so." Ty sighed.

"We'll make sure it does." Chase dropped the towel wrapped around his waist and crawled into bed, settling himself along Tessa's other side. "We'll start now. We'll both hold her and we'll let her pack the bags when she wakes up."

"Sounds good to me." Ty closed his eyes and yawned. "I could do with a nap."

"Wuss."

DECEPTION

THE END

WWW.JENNYPENN.COM

ABOUT THE AUTHOR

I live near Charleston, SC with my two biggies, that's my dogs. I have had a slightly unconventional life. Moving almost every three years, I've had a range of day jobs that included everything from working for one of the worlds largest banks as an auditor, to turning wrenches as an outboard repair mechanic. I've always envied the fact that we only get one life and I have tried to cram as much as I can into this one.

Throughout it all, I've always read books, feeding my need to dream and fantasize about what could be. An avid reader since childhood as a latchkey kid, I'd spend hours at the library earning those shiny stars the librarian would paste up on the board after my name.

I credit my grandmother's yearly visits as the beginning of my obsession with romances. When she'd come, she'd bring stacks of love stories, the old fashion kind that didn't have sex in them. Imagine my shock when I went to the used bookstore and found out what really could be in a romance novel.

I've working on my own stories for years and have found a particular love of erotic romances. In this genre, women are no longer confined to a stereotype and plots are no longer constrained to the rational. I love the anything goes mentality and letting my imagination run wild.

I hope you enjoyed running with me and will consider picking up another book and coming along for another adventure.

Send your comments to Jenny at
jenny@jennypenn.com

MENAGE AMOUR

EXCERPTS

PATTON'S WAY

Cattleman's Club 1

Jenny Penn
Copyright © 2008

STORY EXCERPT

"Now, you know when a man walks in on you fucking yourself and doesn't offer you a hand that he's not interested."

"I don't know." Hailey still hadn't stopped giggling. "Maybe it has something to do with him being your brother."

"Don't start with that crap. Chase is not even my step-brother," Patton corrected quickly. "We're not related."

"Technically, but he probably still thinks of himself as your protector." Hailey belched after making that declaration.

"They're not related to me either, but they still manage to drive me insane with their pompous attitude."

"Pompous." Patton snickered. "I'd say it was more as if it were a God complex. They think they rule the world and we should be happy to be allowed into their kingdom."

"They treat us as if we're still eight."

"Eight-year-olds don't have boobs like these." Patton pointed to her chest.

"Some do. Some of them fashion cover models aren't old enough to drive. Of course, most of them probably aren't virgins by the time they start to drive."

"Gee, thanks, Hailey." Patton gave her friend an insincere smile. "Make me feel better, why don't you?"

"Hey, don't whine to me. You don't have to be a virgin. You could have had the whole alphabet from Adam to Zack if you wanted by now."

"I'm waiting for the right man." Patton began to pick at the label on her bottle, venting her annoyance on the stubborn sticker.

"Technically three men, which makes you the sluttiest virgin I've ever heard of."

"I love Chase, Slade and Devin, but if it isn't to be, I guess I'll find myself three other hunks to gang bang me. God knows there are enough ripped men running around Atlanta to scratch any kind of itch."

"Really? Then why haven't you?"

Patton's shoulders slumped. "I guess I just wanted to be in love with a guy before we had sex."

"That's sweet."

"It's stupid."

"No, it isn't. Following three men around like a love sick puppy when all they do is pat you on the head and tell you 'good, girl', that's stupid."

"I do not follow them around like a puppy."

"Please, spare me. You're the strongest, hard-willed woman I know, but when it comes to the Davis brothers, you turn into some weak, little woman, doing whatever they want, whatever they say."

"I do not!"

"Yeah? So you regularly wear skirts that come down to your ankles and turtle necks all the way up to your chin?"

"Screw you, Hailey."

"Let me ask you this, if it had been any other man than Chase, what would you have done to him for walking out on you like he did today?"

She would have tracked his ass down, pinned him to the wall and ripped him a new one. She might have gone to an adult toy store and bought a pump to send him with a too sweet note apologizing for not recognizing his problem. All sorts of vindictive, mean spirited ideas came to mind.

"That's what I thought."

"I didn't say anything."

"You didn't have to. Your expression said it all. You would have hurt and humiliated the bastard, but what did you do with Chase? Jumped out a window and ran away. Why don't you just keep on running, Patton? Run all the way back to Atlanta, to the life you built there and just admit defeat."

Admit defeat? Never.

* * * *

Both girls were too involved in their conversation to notice Devin moving past the open garden gate or see his head appearing briefly before he ducked back out of sight. Still thinking that they were alone, their conversation went on uncensored.

Devin closed his eyes and banged his head against the fence. He didn't need to hear this. From finding out that she was a virgin, to knowing that she wanted not just one, but all three of them to make her a woman, it was just too much.

The idea that she intended to give up, go to looking for three other men to take her innocence made his blood boil. He didn't direct his anger at Patton though. He aimed it at his two hardheaded brothers for putting them all in this situation.

Patton had been right when she said that they weren't her brothers. They weren't, not by blood, not by marriage, not by law. They were her self-appointed guardians, nothing more.

It had started seventeen years ago. Charley Jones, Patton's father, had worked on the Davis ranch as foreman for as long as anybody could remember. Charley had been best friends with Devin's dad, Mitch.

When Charley's wife just left one day, Devin's mother had pretty much assumed the role of looking after Patton while Charley worked out in the fields. For a mother of three boys, it had been Devin's mom's dream come true to have a little girl to teach to sew and cook.

Then one night, Charley and Mitch had drunk a little too much and gotten into a fight. When the men had been separated, Charley lay dead on the floor from a puncture to the heart.

Mitch had delivered the wound with the knife he always wore strapped to his thigh.

Whatever happened between Mitch and Charley, nobody knew. Mitch had never explained and Charley couldn't. As the cops had walked Mitch out, he had turned to his wife and asked that she look after Patton.

The little six-year-old had moved into the Davis farmhouse and driven Devin insane with her silliness. He had been ten and wanted to be out riding the horses and tending the cattle with his older brothers. Instead, he'd been stuck playing with the pesky little girl.

Forced to play everything from Barbie to dress up, over the years, their relationship had grown from antagonistic to close. When Patton had started to develop, Devin had taken notice. If it hadn't been for Chase and Slade threatening him, he'd have done something about it, too.

Chase and Slade saw her as their little girl lost. They'd played the role of protector to her for so long, they'd refused to accept the notion of her as woman. Slade had always been there helping her with her homework, teaching her how to ride horses and drive a car. Chase had been the father figure, setting curfews and enforcing the rules of the house.

Patton's voice broke through Devin's thoughts. "I refuse to admit defeat."

"Then you're going to die a virgin."

"Maybe that's the problem."

"That's what I've been telling you."

"No, I mean. Maybe if I had some experience, it would help me figure out how to seduce Chase, Slade and Devin."

"It's like watching a horse beat its head into a stall door."

"I'm serious. What I need is a throw away guy."

"A throw away guy?"

"Yeah, a friend with benefits."

"That's never going to work."

"Why not?"

"Because you're not the type of woman."

"I could be."

"You'll fall in love and then be in a worse spot for loving four men."

"Are you going to help or sit there and make pithy little remarks?"

"Fine, you want a throw away guy, I know just the man."

"You do?"

"Trust me on this one. I'll give him a call and we'll get that cherry popped before the end of the week."

Devin took that cue to end this party. He needed to get Patton back home before Chase got there and realized she'd slipped out on him. When he and Slade found out she'd disappeared from her room, they had thought she'd be back before dark.

Then the sun went down and the brothers started to worry. Neither knew what had happened between Chase and Patton, but they knew what Chase would do if he learned about her escape.

Slade had gone off to the club to make sure Chase stayed out while Devin hunted Patton down. Not that it had been hard to find her. There weren't many places in Pittsfield where she could go. Hailey's had been the first on his list.

"Does this hunk come with friends? You know after all these years of fantasizing about being taken by three men at once, I'm not sure only one will do."

"Excuse me," Devin spoke louder than necessary. "It's time to come home, Patton."

His sudden appearance didn't get so much as a squeak of surprise from the two women. They both turned rounded, glazed eyes on him. The empty beer bottles littered around the loungers told him all he needed to know.

"I'm not going anywhere with you, Devin Davis. I'm done with you and your bossy brothers." Patton waggled a finger at him.

"Is that right?" Devin sighed.

"That' right." Patton nodded. "I'm staying here."

"Is that what you think?" Devin didn't falter as he closed in on her.

"That's what I—" Patton's words ended in a shriek as Devin hoisted her over his shoulder. "Damn you, Devin! Put me down!"

"In just a moment, sweetheart." Devin paused long enough to tell Hailey goodnight before he carried his squiggling armload out of the yard and off to his truck.

* * * *

ADULT EXCERPT

The ache in her cunt came to life as a two thick fingers pushed up into her. Patton's eyes popped open with sudden awareness. This was no dream. Two hard, warm male bodies pressed her between them. One leg draped over Slade's thighs left her pussy exposed to his deeply intimate touch while Chase watched with that feral, hungry look in his eyes.

The full thickness of the dildo still filling her ass brought back to vivid life the memories from the past night. She wasn't a virgin anymore. More than that, she was now the Davis brothers' woman.

Chase's hand joined Slade's bringing her back to the present as two more fingers slid into her wet channel. Unwilling to leave any of her untouched, he lowered his head to take one taut nipple into his mouth as Slade took the other into his free hand.

In minutes, they had her moaning and writhing with need. Despite the almost painful stretched sensation in her ass, she rubbed herself against Slade's thick erection hungry to be filled in other ways. Slade chuckled before biting down on her shoulder.

"Sore, baby?" Chase murmured as he pulled his fingers out of her clinging heat to tease the clit hidden at the top of her folds.

"A little," Patton gasped as he played with the bar piercing. "Please."

"Please what, baby?" Chase lifted his head to watch as her head rolled back onto Slade's shoulder, her hips thrusting forward begging for more of the teasing touches they gave her.

"Please, I want…" Patton's words ended in a moan as Slade's finger swirled inside of her, teasing that magical little spot that could shatter her world so effortlessly.

"You want what?" Chase growled. "You want to be fucked?"

"Yes. Oh, God." Patton couldn't control the spasms that had her hips pumping her pussy against Slade's hands.

"Fucked with what? Our fingers, our tongues, or do you want our cocks filling this tight little cunt?"

"Cocks," Patton groaned as their fingers left her.

Her eyes opened but the protest stilled on her lips as she watched Chase line himself up with her wet opening. Slade held her leg higher, giving Chase plenty of room. It filled her with thrills that spiced her pleasure with a darkly erotic element to be fucked by one man while another man held her in position and watched. No doubt, Slade watched.

"Isn't that just the most erotic sight?" Slade's breathed hotly against her ear as Chase slowly fed her clenching pussy one searing inch after another of his silky hardness.

Patton watched with glazed eyes as the blood darkened cock head slipped and disappeared into her much paler flesh. Her swollen cunt lips stretched wide along the width of Chase's erection.

"Look at that pretty, pink pussy glistening with your desire," Slade whispered, his words making her shiver with need and want. "Look how it opens wide to take your lover deep inside you. Tell me, Patton, is he hurting you or is he pleasuring you?"

"Both," Patton groaned.

She spoke the truth. Muscles that had been used for the first time last night ached as they were stretched anew by Chase's thick, hard cock. It was a pleasurable ache, leaving her panting with her need to be full, to have him buried deeply within her body.

"You're to keep that little pussy naked, sweetheart." Slade's deep, husky voice mesmerized her. "I like looking at, like watching it being fucked almost as much as I like fucking into its tight, wet depths. Did you like it, Patton? Did you like it when I fucked you?"

"You know I did," Patton moaned being driven insane by his words and Chase's slow penetration.

"How did it make you feel to know Chase and Devin watched me? To know that I'm watching Chase fuck you now?"

"Hot," Patton gasped as Slade's hands came around to caress and tease her breasts. Instinctively, she arched her back, offering herself up for his teasing.

"You like being watched, don't you?" Slade pulled sharply on her nipples when she failed to respond.

"Yes." Patton had trouble breathing and the word came out choppy and hoarse.

"Yes, what?" Slade demanded with another sharp pull.

"Yes, I like being watched."

"Hmm, I think we should make a new rule then. Maybe we should require you to be naked whenever it's just us. What do you think Chase? Should we keep little Patton naked for our pleasure?"

"Perhaps a little lingerie. A garter belt, stockings and some heels." Chase ground out through clenched teeth.

"And one of those open topped corsets. That way her breasts will always be pushed up and out, ready to be played with. What do you think of that, Patton? Will you make yourself a little outfit for our pleasure?"

"Oh, God," Patton groaned as Chase settled his entire length into her. He paused, his head lowering to nibble along her neck and collarbone. The little nips only added to the delicious pain echoing through her body and she tipped her head back to allow him more access.

"What was that?" One of Slade's hands began to slide down over the quivering muscles of her abdomen to rest at the top of her mound.

"Whatever you want."

"Very good." Slade echoed Chase's chuckle.

"I think she's learning." Slade rewarded her with a single flick of her clit.

"Please," Patton whimpered unable to control the small thrusting movements of her hips as her body begged Slade for another touch, urged Chase to move, anything to relieve the pressure.

"Please what, baby?" Chase continued to leisurely taste her neck.

"Move!" Patton emphasized the demand with a hard jerk of her hips.

"How do you want it, baby?" Chase own hips gave a jerk in response to hers. "Fast and hard or slow and easy?"

"Give it to her hard and fast," Slade answered. "That's what she wants, isn't it, sweetheart?"

"Yes, damnit. Any which way, just fuck me," Patton screeched, drawing another round of chuckles.

"She's cursing." Chase pointed out as he drew slowly back out of her clinging sheath. "She needs more discipline."

"Later. Fuck me first. Discipline me later."

"You can count on it, little one," Chase growled before eliciting a scream of pleasure as he slammed back into her.

He gave it to just as Slade had told him to. Patton bucked and screamed, taking his fierce fuck and returning it thrust for thrust. Her cunt ached a little from all the recent use, her canal stretched to capacity as he violently slammed into her. It felt so good, the sensation nearly driving her over the edge.

Then, as Patton quivered on the brink of orgasm, shaking helplessly with the clenching pre-climax spasms, Chase paused. Patton cried out and thrust her hips desperately against his, trying to force him back onto pace.

Chase couldn't be pressured. When he resumed moving, his strokes remained slow and leisurely causing Patton to snarl at him in frustration.

"You were about to come, baby." Chase smiled smugly. "But I don't remember giving you permission."

"She did that last night with Devin," Slade reminded Chase.

"I guess that's two punishments she earned."

"No, please," Patton whimpered, completely out of her mind with the need to climax.

"I think we need to teach her how to control her climaxes," Chase commented as if he were having a normal conversation.

"Do you want to know how we teach a woman to control her climaxes, Patton?" Slade whispered into her ear.

"Oh, God." Patton didn't want to hear this, knowing instinctively that his words would only add to her already painfully intense desire.

"First we tie her to a bed with her legs spread wide for our pleasure."

"Then," Chase leaned in close to whisper in her other ear, "we bring her to the brink of orgasm again and again and again."

With each word Chase picked up speed until he pounded in and out of her, bringing her right to the verge of the most intense of climaxes.

"Then we stop," Chase matched his actions to his words, "leaving her right there on the edge."

"Please!" Patton screamed unable to stand the teasing anymore.

"That's how we discipline naughty girls who steal climaxes." Chase ignored her desperate cry. "We deny them."

"B-but you de-deny yourselves," Patton stammered trying to think of anything she could do or say to get him to finish what he'd started.

"Oh, no, baby. I can pull out of this tight little cunt and have you finish me off with your beautifully talent mouth. Is that what you want?"

"No," Patton moaned. "Please, don't."

"Why shouldn't he, Patton?" Slade demanded.

"Please, don't leave me like this," Patton wailed. "Let me come."

"All you have to do is ask, baby." Chase kissed her, sealing her cries as he pumped her back up to the pinnacle.

Patton didn't recognize herself anymore. She felt like an animal as she scraped her nails along his back and snarled at him go harder, faster. Her hips fucked him back as hard as he gave it to her.

His balls slapped against her with the force of his movements, pushing her back against Slade's hard length.

Slade's erection had settled into the crease of her ass, pushing against the dildo and making her already tight sheath even tighter.

As she approached the apex, Chase kept going until she fell over the edge in the most amazing rush she'd ever experienced. Hot ecstasy cascaded through her body, leaving nothing untouched by the euphoric flames.

Chase thrust harder against her clenching pussy as he rushed toward his own climax. His great, strong body shuddered as he spilled himself into her depths. Behind her Slade groaned and she felt a second wash of warm liquid bathe her butt cheeks.

Patton would have happily passed back out, was halfway asleep when her two lovers pulled away from her leaving her cold and alone. She blinked open her eyes right before Slade pulled her up from the bed. He turned her in the direction of the bathroom.

"Go get cleaned up. Devin will take out the plug." With that command, he gave her a slap on her ass making the dildo shift and send ripples of pleasured pain through her already over sensitized body.

MENAGE AMOUR

EXCERPTS

DESIRE FOR THREE

Desire, Oklahoma 1

Leah Brooke
Copyright © 2008

She had never had such feelings with any man. Not even her husband had made her feel this way before they got married. Something warmed inside her and she started to feel hope that she wasn't doomed to remain this cold unfeeling creature that she had become.

Looking up at Clay, she felt her nipples harden. He kept glancing at her as he drove, the heat in his gaze unmistakable. She felt the moisture flow from her pussy, amazed again at how much these men affected her.

"We're glad you're coming with us, honey." Folding his much larger hand over hers where they clenched on her thighs, he let his fingers trail over the inside of her thigh, grazing her jeans over her pussy.

"Thank you for giving us a chance to see how good we can be together." His smile told her he knew the effect his hand had on her.

Feeling the need to warn them, Jesse looked straight ahead and began, "I think there's something you should know about me before this goes any further."

"What's that, darlin'?" Rio asked.

"I'm not good at sex," she blurted before she lost her nerve. She continued to stare out the windshield, not having the courage to see the disgust she knew had to be written on their faces. "I don't want you to take it personally, I mean don't blame yourselves if I can't, er, you know." She knew her face turned bright red as she continued to stare straight ahead.

"Come?" Rio asked pleasantly.

"Yes." She nodded. "I usually don't like to be touched. It turns me off. With you, though, it seems to be different, but I'm not used to it." She glanced up at Clay. "I'm not sure what will happen if your touch gets more intimate."

She turned even redder as both men laughed. "Oh, our touch is going to get a helluva lot more intimate," Rio warned.

"Step one," he continued, "seems to be getting you accustomed to our touch. While you're staying with us, will you agree to let us do whatever has to be done to explore your boundaries?"

"Before you answer," Clay added, "be very sure, because if you say yes, you're saying yes to us doing whatever we want to do with you, touching you everywhere. If you truly don't like something, we'll stop, but if you're creaming like you are now, we're going to keep going no matter what you say."

Rio gently turned her to face him, his fingers gentle on her chin. "It's all about your pleasure, honey. Our pleasure depends on your pleasure." She gasped when his thumb caressed her bottom lip. "So, what's it gonna be? Will you agree? Will you trust us with your body, with your pleasure?"

Inhaling deeply, she whispered, "Yes," before she could change her mind. Without thinking, she touched her tongue to Rio's thumb. Startled at herself, she tried to pull back.

"Oh, no, you don't." Rio pulled her onto his lap, her back against his door. "You said yes, and teased me with that little tongue. You're all ours now, darlin'."

With that, he began to kiss her, his tongue sweeping into her mouth in a kiss like none she had ever had before. He tasted like sin as he teased and cajoled with his tongue, urging her to play with him. His fingers pulled up her top and unhooked her bra until her breasts were free for both of them to see.

"Beautiful," she vaguely heard Clay as Rio continued his devious assault. He broke the kiss to pull her top over her head and remove her bra. Running his hands over her breasts, he murmured to Clay, "Feel how smooth and soft she is."

He continued to explore a naked breast while Clay reached over for his own inspection. "Baby, your breasts feel so good, soft here," he circled her breast with his callused hand, "and harder here." He tweaked a nipple, and then pinched it lightly between his thumb and forefinger.

Jesse arched as Clay and Rio continued examining her breasts, lightly pinching and pulling on her nipples as they tried to see what she liked. "Oh, God," she whimpered. Riding along in a truck, half naked while two gorgeous men played with her breasts had to be the most mind blowing experience that she had ever had. Highly aroused, she didn't even care if anyone saw her.

Jesse felt a hand undo the snap on her jeans. Rio kissed her, his hand on her breast as she felt the zipper being lowered. Rio lifted her and she felt her jeans being pulled off. Clad now in only a pair of cotton panties, she felt vulnerable and grew hotter.

She felt a hand, she didn't know whose, and didn't care, lay over her mound. "Your pussy is really wet, sugar." She heard Clay's voice, the tension in it unmistakable. "It's so hot, maybe we better get these panties off."

The way he said "panties" caused her to cream even more. She soon became soaking wet and started to feel a little embarrassed at it. She heard a rip and felt her panties being torn from her. She thought it impossible to get any wetter. She closed her legs as she felt the air from the window on her wet folds.

"Uh, uh," she heard Clay scold. "I want those thighs wide open." Moaning into Rio's mouth, she felt Clay pull her left leg until her foot touched his headrest. Rio meanwhile lifted his mouth from hers and moved her right leg until her foot pushed against the dash board.

With her legs now splayed wide open, Clay had a good view of her pussy. His eyes darkened even further as he reached for her, running his fingers through her soaked folds, then spearing a large finger inside her.

Lying naked, spread wide, with Clay and Rio's undivided attention, she felt more desirable than she had ever felt in her life. They appeared to be mesmerized by everything about her, a balm to a wound she didn't realize was so raw.

She shook so hard with desire now that she would gladly do whatever they asked of her if only they would hurry and do something! She wanted to be fucked as she never had before.

"Please," she whimpered, past caring how wanton she sounded.

"Please, what, baby?" Clay asked deviously.

He knew just what they had done to her, damn it, and more than aware of the effect it had on her. His finger was in her pussy, for Christ sake. He knew the height of her arousal and still he continued to tease her. She moved restlessly on his finger and their wicked grins told her they enjoyed the show.

"You have got to feel how tight she is," Clay told his brother. He pulled his finger out of her and almost immediately she felt another push into her.

She heard Rio moan. "If her pussy is that tight, can you imagine how tight her ass is gonna be?"

"What!" Jesse tried to close her legs to no avail. Both men had a grip on her and she couldn't move anywhere. "I don't do that!"

"Do what, darlin'?" Rio asked. "Don't get fucked in the ass?"

"I've never been taken there," she admitted, then gasped and arched again as Clay touched her clit. "Like that, baby?"

Her mind went blank as Rio continued to stroke her pussy, adding another finger as she heard him tell Clay that she needed to be stretched a little more. She felt the truck stop, and glanced out the window to see that they had pulled up in front of a two story house.

Her eyes closed again as Clay turned in his seat, keeping her legs parted for their touch. He teased her clit mercilessly, circling it until she moved to try to make contact with his finger. He avoided her easily, making her sob in frustration.

"Have you ever had anything in your ass?" Rio asked, hoping her arousal wiped out embarrassment. "A finger, a butt plug, anything?"

"Nooooo! Please, please, please! I'm ready. You don't have to wait."

Rio looked over to see Clay looking as angry as he felt. Remembering what Jesse had told Nat about her sex life, he knew she had never been played with like this. She'd obviously never had this kind of attention, had never been aroused to this extent and they had only just started.

He watched as Clay touched his finger to her clit and gave her what she craved. She arched and came in complete abandon, beautiful as her skin flushed a rosy pink. She screamed, and then whimpered like a kitten as his brother brought her down gently. He wished he could have had his mouth on her but with no room to maneuver in this damn truck he knew that it would have to wait. He would, though, he promised himself. He couldn't wait to get his mouth on that hot pussy.

He had only intended a little petting on the way home, but their little darlin' had gone up in flames. She responded so well to every touch that it surprised him that he hadn't come in his jeans. Watching her come had been more arousing than anything he could remember. Already beautiful to him, when she came she blew him away. He wanted to get his mouth on that pussy. He loved to eat pussy, and since he and Clay had all but claimed her for their own, his desire to taste her grew even stronger.

He couldn't imagine anything better than the taste of his woman's pussy.

He wanted to shove his cock inside her so deep that she would feel it in her throat. But, as tight as she felt, he and Clay would have to be gentle with her as they stretched her to accept them. They would get Jesse so hot, she would beg them to fill her.

Rio strode into the master bedroom and noticed Clay pulling down the bedding with a flick of his wrist. He looked down at the tempting bundle in his arms, completely naked, her skin flushed a rosy hue, and grimaced as his jeans became even more uncomfortable.

Laying his precious bundle on the cool, crisp sheets, he stood and tore off his clothing, his eyes never leaving the beautiful woman on the bed. Jesse eyes widened as she watched them undress, starting to look a little nervous as she saw them naked for the first time.

Rio saw how Jesse's eyes moved back and forth as she watched him and his brother undressing. He couldn't wait to sink into her, any part of her, and he knew by the look on his brother's face, that he felt the same.

But, after hearing what that bastard of an ex-husband had put her through in the bedroom, he knew they would have to go slowly; arouse her again thoroughly until she begged to be taken.

Clay shifted, drawing Rio's attention and, out of Jesse's sight, reminded his brother with a gesture that they had to slow down. Rio nodded and took a deep breath before reaching for her.

* * * *

Jesse could hardly believe this. She had just had the most incredible orgasm of her life, still weak from it as she watched Clay and Rio undress. She shifted, uncomfortably aware of how wet she was and embarrassed. She wanted a few minutes alone.

She asked the only thing that came to mind. "Can I take a shower?"

"Later, baby," Clay promised. "Rio and I will give you a bath."

No one had bathed her since she'd been a little girl and she wasn't sure she would be comfortable with being bathed by Clay and Rio. But all thoughts of a bath went out of her head as they finished undressing.

Dressed, they were intimidating. Naked, they were lethal. She knew that both Clay and Rio were older than her own almost forty years, but not an inch of flab could be seen on them anywhere. Years of working their ranch showed in the way their muscles shifted as they moved.

Clay removed his boxers and Jesse's eyes widened as she took in his size. She wondered frantically how she would be able to accept him into her body. He looked thicker than her wrist and long. She had thought of Brian as average, but he was tiny compared to Clay.

She glanced over as Rio's boxers came off and moaned. Almost as thick as Clay, his cock looked even longer.

"I don't think this is going to work," she blurted nervously.

Clay and Rio looked at each other and smiled at her reassuringly.

"We're going to fit inside you like a hand in a glove, baby," Clay promised as he brushed her cheek with his thumb and moved in, taking her lips in a kiss so possessive and hungry it curled her toes.

Clay's kiss proved to be just as intoxicating as Rio's, but where Rio's lips had been teasing, Clay's demanded. His tongue swept through her mouth, tangling with hers, possessively exploring, demanding a response Jesse couldn't withhold.

He lifted his head to gaze at her hungrily. Jesse lifted her hands to his dark hair, grasping handfuls of its thick silkiness, absently tracing her thumbs over where she knew a few strands of silver shone.

As he lowered his head to her breast, scraping her nipple with his sharp teeth, she felt Rio move between her thighs.

She sucked in a breath as Clay nipped and sucked at her breasts, using his lips, his tongue and his teeth, thoroughly exploring them, seeming to gauge her response to every touch.

Rio parted her folds with his thumbs, making her squirm. She didn't think it possible to get aroused again so soon after having such a mind-blowing orgasm.

"I'm gonna lap up this sweet pussy, darlin'," she heard him say even as she felt him part her further, her legs over his broad shoulders, keeping them open.

Clay paused and looked over his shoulder and watched Rio lower his head to Jesse's pussy. He heard Jesse's gasp as she jolted in his arms when Rio's tongue swept through her folds. He watched her eyes glaze over with passion as Rio used his mouth, thoroughly exploring the woman that they had been looking for all their lives.

He heard Rio moan and knew his brother was enjoying his first taste of their woman. He felt Jesse writhe in his arms as Rio used his mouth on her, smiling when he saw his brother slide his hands under her bottom and lift her more firmly against his mouth.

Clay moved to kneel on the bed, one hand stroking his throbbing cock and with the other he reached out to cup Jesse's cheek. When she looked at his cock and licked her lips, his cock jumped.

"I want my cock in your mouth," he told her.

She gasped, opening her mouth and Clay moved closer.

"Will you teach me how?" she asked, looking up at him.

Clay saw Rio lift his head and knew that he'd heard her, too. When Jesse smiled at him shyly he felt his cock jump again.

"Baby, have you ever had a cock in your mouth?"

"No. I never wanted Brian that way."

"Open your mouth, baby." Clay rubbed the head of his cock on her lips. He wanted to push himself all the way into her hot mouth. Knowing that he would be the first almost set him off but he gritted his teeth against it and soon had himself under control, barely.

"Darlin'," he heard Rio as he pushed the head of his cock between her soft lips, "Has anybody but me tasted this sweet pussy?"

Clay moaned as Jesse shook her head, her mouth rubbing against the head of his cock. He looked over to see the incredulous pleasure on Rio's face. He knew just what his brother was thinking. Jesse's sexuality had barely been tapped. The woman writhing helplessly under their hands and desperately trying to suck his cock into her untutored mouth had almost no sexual experience.

It would be up to them to teach her everything. She had been fucked, but never taken in the ways that Clay and Rio planned to take her. She was aroused, but it was nothing next to what they would do to her. She had never been fussed over the way they wanted to pamper her, and she had never had her man spank her if she disobeyed them.

All the things they had done with women over the years would be brand new again as they taught their woman. She belonged to them.

Her hot mouth drove him crazy. He'd become too aroused with his cock in her mouth for the first time to be able to show her anything, and this time he didn't need to anyway. What she didn't have in experience she more than made up for in enthusiasm.

Clay felt ecstatic that she responded so well to them. He'd become so aroused by their woman that he struggled to maintain some kind of control when he wanted nothing more than to devour her whole. Glancing at Rio, he saw that his brother appeared just as taken with her.

Jesse felt Rio position himself at her entrance and trembled in anticipation. She wanted him inside her so badly, wanted them both more than she could ever dream she'd want a man.

She took as much of Clay's cock into her mouth as she could and tried to squirm onto Rio's but he held her still.

"I'm gonna fuck this hot little pussy, darlin'."

She heard Rio's voice over the loud groans that filled the room and wished he would hurry. His shallow thrusts gained ground with each thrust but she wanted it all.

Now!

Jesse had never felt so wanted in her life, had never felt so feminine as she took Clay's and Rio's cocks. Clay's taste filled her with heat and she couldn't get enough of it. His response to having her mouth on him drove her wild.

She felt powerful and wicked as she used her tongue on him and tried to suck him as far as she could into her mouth. She heard his moans and felt his hands tighten on her as she sucked him deep, wanting him to lose the control she knew he was trying so desperately to hold on to.

She arched as Rio fucked her. She couldn't prevent the constant moans coming from deep in her throat as Clay and Rio drew responses from her that had lay dormant for years.

Every inch of her body hummed. She arched, forcing Rio's cock further into her dripping pussy and groaned at the fullness.

"Easy, darlin'," he said from between clenched teeth. "I don't want to hurt you."

She squirmed restlessly and sucked harder at Clay. She burned and needed more and tried to move but Clay and Rio easily controlled her.

She felt Clay tighten and try to pull away. She sucked harder and scraped her teeth warningly over his cock, ignoring his tense "Fuck!" Her hands tightened on him, one holding the base of his cock, not allowing him to pull away and the other cupping the full sack between his thighs.

She felt his fists tighten in her hair. "Baby, I'm gonna come. Let go," he growled.

As Rio pushed his full length into her, Jesse doubled her efforts and she heard Clay moan.

"Fuck," she heard Clay bite out as he filled her mouth with his seed. Swallowing frantically, she continued to suck every bit from him as he stroked her hair.

"You're amazing, baby," he crooned, pulling out of her mouth to move beside her on the bed. He leaned over to kiss her, his lips biting hers erotically. "You are going to be punished for not letting go when I told you to, though. Rio and I want to watch you come again, baby. You belong to us now, don't you? Give it to us."

Jesse heard Clay's words as Rio pushed deeper inside her. The full feeling had her trembling helplessly.

"Darlin', you feel fantastic," Rio groaned. "You're so tight!"

"Harder!" Jesse pleaded. She was so close. As Rio continued his slow smooth strokes, Clay's mouth on her breasts tormented her further.

"I don't want to hurt you, darlin'." Rio held her hips firmly in his strong hands, not allowing her to push his cock deeper as she writhed, desperate to come.

Her clit throbbed. When she felt Clay's hand cover her abdomen, she whimpered.

"Please! I need more. Touch me!"

Clay lifted his head and his eyes met hers. She saw the tenderness in their depths as she felt his fingers move lower.

She knew when Rio's control finally snapped. His thrusts became harder. His hands tightened on her hips. He buried himself to the hilt inside her, his cock hitting her womb. She came in a fierce orgasm that wrung a scream from her, frightening her with its intensity. She dimly heard Rio groan as he pounded into her.

"Fuck," he panted. "Her pussy's milking my cock. So fucking hot!"

He surged into her with one last powerful thrust, holding her hips firmly in place as she felt Clay's touch on her sensitive clit.

"No more! No more!" Shaking her head weakly, she lifted her hand toward Clay. She felt Rio's pulsing cock splash his seed deep inside her as Clay's fingers moved on her clit.

"Once more, baby," she heard Clay croon. Grasping her outstretched hand firmly in his, he and Rio wrung another rippling orgasm from her.

Siren Publishing, Inc.
www.SirenPublishing.com

Printed in the United States
151330LV00012BA/62/P